BITTER BLOOD

Jack Stallard was the classic gun loner, yet with no fear of loneliness. He truly believed in justice and when it could not be meted out by a judge on his high bench then he, Jack Stallard, was there to deliver it hot and final from the barrel of a Colt .45. Now he was on the track of a vicious killer and an unprincipled bounty hunter. How Jack finally gets his man and restores peace to a troubled land provides a compulsively readable yarn of the old West.

BITTER BLOOD

by

Clint Ryker

Dales Large Print Books
Long Preston, North Yorkshire,
BD23 4ND, England.

British Library Cataloguing in Publication Data.

Ryker, Clint
    Bitter blood.

    A catalogue record of this book is
    available from the British Library

    ISBN   978-1-84262-652-8 pbk

First published in Great Britain 2007 by Robert Hale Limited

Copyright © Clint Ryker 2007

Cover illustration © Gordon Crabb by arrangement with
Alison Eldred

Published in Large Print 2008 by arrangement with
Robert Hale Limited

Dales Large Print is an imprint of Library Magna Books Ltd.

Printed and bound in Great Britain by
T.J. (International) Ltd., Cornwall, PL28 8RW

CHAPTER 1

PAY A KILLER'S DUES

Jack Stallard followed the killer's trail to Dog City and across the Blackwood Mountains then onwards to Sunset Mesa, Gant, Big Fork and Murphy's Wells. A lot of towns and a lot of miles, yet as he dusted towards Trinidado on Rogue River he knew Bo Gaunt was slowing down at last.

The tall horseman with the wide shoulders, the black leathern shirt and the tied-down Colt .45s encountered a whiskery old-timer on the edge of town, reined in.

'Good day, old man.'

'Howdy, stranger.'

'I'm looking for a man.'

The old-timer looked uneasy. Squinting up at the rider silhouetted against the shimmering Territory sun, he scented trouble in him like you could with a maverick horse. The veteran had seen unsmiling loners like this show up often enough during his long years in vast Calico Valley. Likely too often.

Most times when they finally rode out they left somebody weeping.

His throat felt dry as dust. He cleared it noisily and attempted a grin. 'And who might this here feller be, stranger?'

'Bo Gaunt is the name. Tall and well-made and sports a pencil-line moustache.'

'Afraid I don't recall nobody tallying with that there description, mister.'

Stallard stared at the man so long and hard he first dropped his head, then began fidgeting uneasily. He eventually found the courage to mutter, 'Got to be getting on,' and shuffled away.

Stallard watched him out of sight. Only then did he switch his gaze to play slowly over sun-stricken Trinidado, seeing everything, missing nothing. The oldster had been lying, of course. He had seen it clearly in his rheumy old eyes. But why should the man lie – unless Gaunt was still here, maybe someplace close by, even?

The gunfighter shook his head. This just didn't figure somehow. He'd cut down on the killer's head start plenty since setting out after him a week back after he'd been on a killing rampage. First he'd gunned down a state governor in Reno, and, while escaping, he'd strangled a banker's wife in Milestone,

Utah. Then he'd taken to the owlhoot trail and had shot a leading jeweller with important friends while robbing a wagon train. A huge bounty had been put on his head, and Stallard was dead set that he was the one to collect it. Yet Gaunt still retained as much as a twenty-hour lead. It simply didn't figure that scum like that would dally for any reason when he could still run.

He rode on down Main.

Trididado comprised a long rough stem street fronted by dusty buildings, intersected twice by cross-streets. There was a saloon, a general store, a stage depot and a big new emporium that catered to the immigrant wagon trains which were a regular feature rumbling into Calico Valley that summer.

Three horses stood hipshot out front of the Red Bull saloon switching flies with their tails. There was nobody to be seen in any direction. The saloon's batwings were propped open to take full advantage of whatever wisp of breeze might happen along when Jack Stallard swung down, tied up and walked in.

The Red Bull smelt like it had housed one recently. The place was dim and hot with sawdust on the floor and one mangy yellow hound asleep on a bench against the wall.

Three men sat playing stud at a table. They looked up sharply at the jingle of spurs then quickly returned their attention to their cards. Too quickly. Stallard eyed them coldly. They had the hardcase look, he saw. His cold eyes flicking from face to face, Stallard felt the old familiar tingle in his wrists, that surge or sureness go through his body.

He sniffed.

He could smell trouble in the Red Bull saloon, but couldn't yet scent any whiff of Bo Gaunt.

The barkeep was fat and frightened. His name was Henry Dolan and he kept glancing across at the card-players as he made his reluctant way along the bar.

'Yeah?'

'Sourmash.'

'Fifteen cents.'

'That's too much for whiskey. I'll pay ten.'

Dolan shot Stallard a sick look, poured the liquor and scooped up the proffered ten cents. As he was turning away, he hissed, 'Skee-daddle out of here, mister. Them boys are laying for you.'

Stallard's strong-boned features reflected no change as he lifted the brimming glass to his lips and stared into the dark bar mirror to see three pairs of eyes drilling into his back like augers.

He lowered his glass and spoke loudly. 'I'm looking for a man named Bo Gaunt, barkeep.'

Dolan directed another frantic message at him with his eyes, but Stallard ignored it.

'My name is Jack Stallard,' he went on. He spoke more softly now yet his words reached every corner of the room. 'I am looking for Gaunt to kill him.'

Silence fell, total and deep. Then the gunfighter turned with slow deliberation to face the hardcases squarely as they rose together and began to fan out. Stallard's left hand fingered back his flat-brimmed hat, his right dropped casually close to his gun.

'I wouldn't try it, gents,' he warned, sounding almost avuncular. 'You see, I'm a professional and you're amateurs – real amateurs, if I'm any judge. So it just could play out more like a massacre than a gunfight if you were to start anything.'

They stared unblinking. He let that word 'massacre' sink in before he went on.

'So, what's the score? Gaunt pay you to take me out of the game?' He saw his words hit home in stubbled and ugly faces. 'Yeah, guess that sounds like Gaunt right enough. Likely paid you handsome for taking on this real dangerous job of work, too. He was well-heeled when he quit Decatur City – just ahead of that big posse.'

Blaise Cardiff was a thick-necked waddy, heavy in shoulder and gut, a small-town brute with a reputation. Waiting until Jarrett and Cade had positioned themselves wide on either side of him, he hitched his heavy shell-belt up around his drum gut and spoke round an unlit stogie.

'We just happen to know you're just a low back-shooter, Stallard.' His voice sounded like a guitar strummed inside a tin shed. 'Mr Gaunt warned you'd likely try and spread a whole mess of lies about him.'

Stallard's eyes tightened.

'You'd be better off listening to me than him, mister. That way you might just get to stay alive!'

'Unbuckle that gunrig or make use of it, back-shooter!' Cardiff cut him off, meaty hand hovering over gunbutt. 'We don't aim to waste good time jawboning with the likes of your sneaky breed!'

Stallard's face went completely blank, mirroring the blankness inside him. Hard as he might be, he would mostly offer any man a chance to save his life, but was always ready to play the game hard if they failed to take up his offer. He decided he had no more reason to go easy with this one than he would have for a woman-killer like Bo Gaunt.

His tone dropped a notch. 'Get your hand away from that gun, or use it!'

For just a moment tough Blaise Cardiff felt a stab of uncertainty – despite what he'd been told about Gaunt's pursuer being just a second-rater. Then that moment was gone and he was suddenly ready to earn his easy one hundred dollars.

He cursed and grabbed gun handle.

Nobody even saw Stallard come clear. One moment he was standing there before the grimy bar with both hands empty, the next his right hand was filled with a bellowing Colt .45 that shook the saloon with its cannon blast and slammed three bullets into Cardiff's barrel chest, jarring the badman from head to heels and knocking him down hard to expire with a last piggish grunt of shock and disbelief.

The smoking Colt swung on Jarrett, who flung both empty hands at the ceiling and then gave way at the knees from simple funk. At his side an ashen Cade covered his big-nosed face with both hands as though in pathetic defence from the shots he expected, but which never came.

Stallard sneered as he lowered the smoking weapon. How well he knew this breed! Drygulchers, cowards and scum, every one. The kind who'd kill an old man or woman quick as a blink, yet rarely had the stomach for anything that might carry a whiff of real danger.

Times like this he felt almost like a vastly superior breed of gunfighter by comparison. Almost...

'How much did Gaunt pay you?'

'One hundred each,' Jarrett panted.

'Reckon it was worth it now?'

Two pairs of glazed eyes focused on the dead man. Uncomely in life, the beefy figure was grotesque in death. He was leaking blood like a slaughtered steer.

The room was now cathedral-quiet as they stared fixedly at the man with the still smoking gun. They still weren't sure if they would survive.

'No ... please no,' Cade panted. Then suddenly the man seemed genuinely offended. 'God damn it all! Gaunt lied to us. He swore on his mother's life that you were just some tenth-rater–'

'Is he still in Trinidado?'

'No,' Jarret answered, and there could be no doubting he spoke the truth now. 'He quit town last night, making for Chad City.'

'He mean to hole up there?' Stallard snapped.

'He never said, mister,' Cade supplied. 'But he did say as how he figgers Chad City is about to boom big now that Calico Valley's been thrown open to them homesteaders from the East.'

Stallard nodded to himself and began refilling the Colt from his shell-belt.

During the manhunt he'd overtaken scores of lurching prairie schooners lumbering along half-made trails leading into Calico Valley, great shuddering monsters of canvas-covered ugliness laden down with children, furniture and hope.

A sourdough he'd met at Rebel River told him there had already been serious clashes in the valley between the incumbent cattle kings and all these swarming newcomers.

This was usual in such cases and places, he knew from experience. The beef barons didn't mean to stand by and watch their kingdoms carved up into forty-acre leases, while the newcomers were so hardened by poverty and privation they were ready to fight and even die for that which they had been convinced were their just rights to their share of the Great West.

Yet all this historic upheaval meant to the man of the gun was that the Calico Valley he envisioned would surely boast at least one major boom town which would doubtless offer a dozen kinds of trouble, loose money and the prospect of anonymity for a killer such as Gaunt. He further figured that Gaunt, having hired three gunners to kill him here, might be dumb enough to rest up some in Calico Valley now, thinking he was safe. If that was the case it might prove the biggest mistake that heller ever made.

He turned his back on Jarret and Cade and holstered the gun. Spurs chimed softly as he quit the room. He paused a moment on the porch, staring across the street at the scatter of townspeople drawn by the gunfire, then went to his horse.

It was forty miles to Chad City.

'Judd Steever, just what are you doing back there?'

'Huh? Oh ... just sluicing the mud off me, Em. Be with you in a minute.'

Next moment the young woman seated on the high seat of the battered Conestoga wagon which had carried the three cousins all the vast way down from Salt Lake City, Utah, to their promised land of Calico Valley, clearly heard the distinct clink of a bottle.

Emma Green pressed her hands together tightly, then let them lie like tired lovers in her lap, fearing for a bad moment that she might have reached breaking-point.

She fought the feeling with all her strength, and eventually, as always, the self-discipline which was as much a part of her as her fine dark tresses and steady grey eyes, won through.

Gathering herself together, she dragged her gaze away from the dreary familiarity of wagon and team and instead turned to take in the lovely green vistas of Calico Valley. While one of her cousins sought whatever strength he might find from his whiskey, before full night came down on them.

The family wagon stood on the west bank of Eagle Feather Creek, ten miles to the east of Chad City. Until the previous day the cousins had been part of the wagon train they'd first joined way back in Kansas. Yesterday they'd been forced to fall back when Judd Steever got so drunk he'd become unable to drive.

Along with cousin Jasmine – who was virtually no help at all – they had just spent several hours digging the wagon out of a riverside bog, which Emma knew could

15

easily have been avoided had they been still travelling with wagon train boss Charlie Bowdre and the others. Instead she found herself at that moment, wet, muddy, exhausted and exasperated, yet still with no intention of quitting.

She would see the journey through to Chad City where she knew things would be better. They simply had to be.

'Come on, Judd,' she called, her voice flat and toneless. She was a little afraid, she knew. But aware of Judd's weakness, she knew she must not show it and run the risk of adding to his anxiety. She raised her voice and called, 'We're moving on, Jasmine!' She slid across and patted the driver's seat to make a space for the gangling young man. 'Do hurry.'

Judd Steever faked a resolute expression and crossed to the rig to raise one muddied boot to a wagon stirrup. He heaved himself into the driver's seat. He lifted the reins but wasn't yet ready to motion the teamers forward.

He was scared of the river, his cousin saw. That did not surprise her. He had been scared ever since their first glimpse of a genuinely wild redskin outlined majestically against a high plains sunset some two weeks earlier.

'Some sweet country, eh, Emma?' He forced a smile. 'Sure never expected the land of opportunity to look this good, did you?'

Emma made no reply. She was watching the changing colours in the sky and the way an uncertain wind ruffled the surface of the river. She was far too weary to enthuse about anything at the moment yet was aware that Calico Valley was indeed an incredibly beautiful place. Even so, she would have infinitely preferred to be back in Utah in Salt Lake City surrounded by hundreds of fine homes and lamplit streets with policemen walking their beats and endless miles separating her from Eagle Feather Creek.

She studied the man at her side with a sidelong glance, her brow puckered in thought. She was wondering yet again if her decision for them to quit Salt Lake City and venture south might yet prove to have been a grievous mistake and error of judgement.

Then she reminded herself they'd really been left with little option.

Back home, dictatorial and ailing old Uncle Hector had made it only too plain he wanted his younger kinfolk to go off and strike out for the frontier and make something of themselves, leaving him free either to die in peace or to go on chasing women day and night as he had been doing ever since his wife was mercifully called to her Reward.

He'd made the Territory sound almost glamorous. He'd bought property in a place called Chad City as an investment which he'd eventually bequeathed to nieces and nephew when the medicos warned him he might be fast approaching that time when he would pinch the rosy bottom of his last chorus girl.

Brother and sister Judd and Jasmine Steever agreed to take advantage of his generosity and made their preparations to leave for the south, but could not find the final courage to do so until a reluctant Cousin Emma agreed to accompany them. Her involvement in the enterprise had been finally secured only by her uncle's handsome retainer – which at times she felt she'd earned a dozen times over long before they got to within a hundred miles of their destination.

Judd had been drinking more and more heavily by the day and boasting wildly about the great fortune they would make eventually, which was his way of dealing with the fact that he was scared as hell.

Cousin Jasmine was far tougher and matter of fact than her brother, but those qualities didn't make her an ideal travelling companion. The contrary, in truth.

Emma was reminded afresh of just how unhelpful her cousin could be when Jasmine eventually joined herself and Judd, then immediately started in complaining about the flies.

Flies were the least of their problems on the frontier. They came far behind the threat of Indian raids, outlaws, stampeding buffalo herds – or getting lost.

Yet despite everything Emma remained as committed as ever. She had promised Uncle Hector she would see all three of what remained of his blood kin settled safely in Nevada, and that she would do.

'What do you reckon, Em?'

She turned to Judd, her gaze blank for a moment. 'Pardon?'

He nodded at the big river they were flanking. 'Time to look for a crossing, you think?'

They both looked to her for leadership. That was flattering but could be a burden. What would she know about crossing rivers?

She forced herself to concentrate. The Eagle Feather here was broad-bosomed and smooth-running, but she'd remembered that while with the train they'd mostly done their river crossings where rocks and shale were visible.

'I think we should drive south a little further, Judd,' she suggested. 'Either that or...'

She broke off as a sound reached them. Turning sharply, all three immediately sighted the two riders approaching through the gloom from the north, following the course of the river towards their position. Both men were large, dark and surly-looking. Immediately she felt the bite of uncertainty. If only they hadn't lost touch with the wagon train!

'It's all right, girls,' Judd Steever reassured. He drew back his shoulders and squared his jaw. 'Don't you worry, I can take care of this, whatever it is they want.'

It quickly became plain that what the riders from a nearby ranch to the north wanted was for the 'nesters' to turn their wagon around and head back the way they had come. The men claimed both this section of river and the land beyond to be the titled property of their employer and boss of Slash K ranch.

The young women glanced at Judd. He was looking away. Emma set her chin and turned back to the riders.

'We happen to know we are crossing freehold land. We have the right to camp here, even stake a claim, and have maps to prove it. Now be on your way and let's have no more of this rubbish.'

These were hardcases quite capable of dealing with hick wagoners. But such was Emma Green's composure and self-assurance that the pair faltered, glanced uncertainly at one another, then wheeled and went kicking back the way they had come.

'You'll be right sorry you never done what we said!' one yelled back. 'Mr Potter hates you stinking nesters worse than swallowing goat purge, and that's a fact.'

'Damned sorry!' affirmed his companion, and they lashed their mounts into a furious gallop to be swiftly swallowed by the encroaching gloom.

'Gee, girls, I'm sorry I–'

'It's all right, Judd,' Emma said, trying not to sound sharp. 'Come on, we might as well make camp right where we are.'

'What about those men?' Jasmine asked uncertainly. She was blonde in contrast to Emma's dark beauty, buxom where her older cousin was dagger-slim.

'Just wild boys playing games,' Emma said emphatically, stepping down. 'Come on, you take care of the horses, Judd, and we'll fix supper.'

'Sure, cousin, whatever you say.'

'A penny for your thoughts, Emma.'

'Pardon?'

'You were miles away just then.'

Emma Green blinked in the fireglow and came back slowly to the here-and-now – the river, the starlight and the great uncertainty of their future.

'Oh, I guess I was just wondering how we'll make out in Chad City,' she lied.

Judd Steever made an expansive gesture.

'Make out? Why, we'll set that town right on its ear, that's for sure. From what we've been hearing all the way west, land values are jumping like crazy, there's at least six saloons to every block, and, best of all, we won't have old Unc Hector around to embarrass us.'

'Do you think he really went to all that trouble to get rid of us just in order that he might feel free to chase harlots around the streets?' Jasmine asked.

'I'm sure they weren't *all* ladies of the night, honey,' Emma said. Then she smiled. 'Although, when I think of the ones I actually saw, then maybe...'

It was only when she stopped speaking that her companions heard the sound she had just detected in the growing darkness – the thud of hoofbeats.

CHAPTER 2

TROUBLE ON THE RIVER

It was dirty weather when Stallard awoke in a tree-lined canyon west of the stage route, a dark and sullen climate change rolling in from the south. With the afternoon light beginning to fade from the sky and the surrounding grasses alternately shivering then becoming stock-still, he only had to gaze off at the distant hills to see that big black cloud approaching fast before a sharpening wind.

Yet paradoxically he rubbed his unshaven jaw with something like relish and there was a distinct lift in his step as he strode across to the horse. The way he figured, the combination of a hangover and threatening weather should keep his thoughts from lingering on what had happened the previous day.

Even those who claimed to know him well didn't realize that there were times when this gunfighter's profession could bite back at him, bringing on periods of regret and self-recrimination even when he'd spilled guilty blood to save innocent lives.

He was impressed to realize he'd slept the entire afternoon away; nothing like rest to clear a man's thinking and set him back on course.

No more regrets.

Get up. Get going. Get over it.

Soon he was long-striding through heavy timber, leading the red stallion. Thin rain spattered his face but he just sleeved it away and grinned, an almost handsome, faintly scarred man of thirty with eyes that had maybe seen too much yet with a wide and generous cut of a mouth that rarely smiled.

Stallard was the classic gun loner, yet with no fear of loneliness. For he was content with his own company, had been ever since a childhood he never spoke of. His mind and gunspeed made him strong. Those men he stood against – the ruthless, the rich and the murderous – rarely knew anything about him. Yet he knew them all for what they were and what they were capable of doing in the name of power and greed. Just as he knew what their fate might well be should they cross with him.

The man of the gun was not without his own morality. For he truly believed injustice, whether it be meted out by a judge on his high bench, or came hot and final from the barrel of a Colt .45.

He was as the West had made him and he rode south in the high summer of 1868 with twin revolvers riding his hips and with a name on his mind.

Bo Gaunt. Killer.

For a solid two hours he continued to bull his way on foot through thinning forests, deliberately punishing himself while making it easy on the horse which had already covered vast miles to bring him to Trinidado and his rendezvous with that lone killer.

He paused briefly to take a generous swig from his water canteen, then a remedial jolt from the flask. He sleeved his lips and glanced up at piled-up cloud masses and listened to the wind chattering like a telegraph key in the branches of the dead tree directly overhead. He realized that the weather was being blown away with the promise of blue skies.

It was working. The big lonesomeness and the improving weather were bringing him back to where he'd been before the last gunfight.

Absently he stroked the stallion's neck. Red responded by trying to bite off a finger or two. But the man's reflexes were far too sharp for that, and the horse was forced to rear back when his fingertips flipped its muzzle.

'Seems like you're rested up enough.' He grinned, and threw himself into the saddle, kicked once then set the horse to a long rising slope.

Eventually he cut sign that told him he was leaving the wild country behind and moving back into semi-settled regions. In bright sun-ight now, he saw where several riders had passed over yonder where a faint trace of trail showed; a single traveller had made camp in the lee of that giant grey boulder yonder.

He reined in sharply upon emerging from the timberline a mile further on. Below him lay a vast valley huddled beneath afternoon sunlight, pure and golden.

There were horsemen down there, sitting their saddles in a circle with wafts of tobacco smoke clinging to their indistinct figures.

Stallard fingered gunbutt, his jaw-muscles working. He didn't know who they might be – cowboys, vigilantes, lawmen or just drifters. These days, a man might run across any of those breeds – or all four within the space of just one day's ride.

After a time he decided they seemed harm-less enough. So he pushed on, taking a more southerly track to avoid making contact. In the wake of violence he was often inclined to seek a period of peace and solitariness until he was whole within himself again.

By the time he'd put another mile behind him he was rocking easy in the saddle and drawing luxuriously on a freshly lit stogie.

On a level stretch he halted to give the horse a blow. The fading day was growing cooler and his thoughts were of a snug saloon, a double shot of rye in his fist and maybe someone soft for a little company. He kicked his mount forward and followed a faint trace of trail that eventually brought him to a bald hill which afforded a panoramic view of countryside, river, and in the far distance the smokes of a sizeable town.

Chad City, his destination, he guessed.

Then he saw it.

A mile distant where the Eagle Feather River transcribed a wide and graceful curve in its southward course, a Conestoga and team – small at this distance through the rising mists – stood hauled up by the riverbank. Focusing his gaze he could make out someone moving about, but that was all. No telling whether they might be male or female, but it appeared to him that they might be trying to decide whether they should attempt to ford the river.

His decision, in their shoes, would be to move on a couple of miles further south to the shallows. The crossing was far easier there. There was something about the look of that rig that told him the personnel could well be westbounders, which out here was just another word for nesters.

He shrugged unconcernedly and was heeling forward when further movement caught the corner of his eye. To the north he glimpsed two riders following the course of the Eagle Feather south in the direction of the wagon and team in the deepening twilight. When he brought the two into closer view a mile further down, he thought they looked vaguely familiar, then guessed they could be from that bunch he'd sighted earlier upriver. He realized they were making directly for the Conestoga.

The hair on the back of his neck lifted. He sniffed, and caught the whiff of trouble.

He immediately told himself that whatever might be playing out down there in the deepening gloom, it had nothing to do with Jack Stallard.

And yet he continued to sit his horse as darkness crept across the land and a brave little campfire showed down at the wagon camp.

He pictured those horsemen he'd seen, then shook their image from his mind and turned his horse away.

The red horse was just breaking into a lope when the bellow of a heavy rifle shattered the evening's quiet.

With supper over the westbounders sat over coffee by the fire discussing plans for their new life in Chad City. The rain was gone, the night now velvet-dark with big western stars gleaming in the vaulted arch of the sky.

Emma linked her hands around her knee and smiled at some remark Judd made. Hoot owls sounded further up the slopes and later a badger came right into the firelight, sniffed at them suspiciously then swaggered off with such a comical rolling gait that all three laughed.

It was as the laughter died away that there came the steady thud of hoofbeats. Immediately they jumped to their feet, eyes probing the moon-misted surrounds.

'Better get into the wagon, girls,' Judd said shakily, trying to be a man. 'This could be trouble.'

Quickly Jasmine ran for the wagon. But Emma stood her ground. Judd appeared ready to take flight also, but the sight of

Emma standing there very upright and looking unflustered steadied him some. Then he started easing crabwise to where his .32 rested against the wagon's front wheel, until the ugly crash of a rifle breached the hush and a slug slammed the wheel mere inches from him, causing him to turn rigid with alarm.

'All right, nesters!' a big voice yelled. 'Just freeze and don't try nothing!'

They stood motionless and moments later the two riders emerged from the rapidly deepening darkness beyond a big old oak. One was tall and grizzled with high shoulders, an unlit cigarette dangling from the corner of his mouth. His companion was younger, with black curly hair and an air of arrogant self-assurance.

The tall one was grim and hostile but his companion flashed a cocky grin as they reined in by the fire.

'Well, damnitall, but this is sure some cosy-looking set-up, wouldn't you say, Dock?'

The man called Dock nodded, his eyes never leaving Judd, as though he was hoping he would make another move for the Winchester.

The younger rider leaned forward against the pommel and pushed his hat further back to reveal even more glossy curls. 'Sorry about that shot, feller.' He grinned, not sounding sorry at all. 'But it worked, eh?' He paused to wink at Emma. 'I mean, it saved me and old mossyhorn Dock here having to shoot nobody, right?'

'What do you want?' Emma demanded. 'Who are you?'

'Curly Blazer is my name, and chasing nesters is my game,' came the flip reply. 'Hey, Dock, you hear that? Just made a rhyme. I said Curly–'

'I heard, I heard,' cut in Dock Ollinger. 'Let's just cut the gab and get on with it, Curly.'

Curly Blazer was suddenly not grinning any longer. 'Get on with it? Good thinking.' His stare drilled hard at Emma as he straightened in the saddle. 'Our boss is a big rancher here-abouts who's lately been having a power of trouble with folks just like you showing up out of noplace and trying to homestead his land and acting like you plan to stay around. But that don't suit, *compre?* He wants you gone and me and crabby old Dock here are gonna see that happen or someone is going to get hurt. Make myself plain?'

'Do you work for Mr Potter?' Emma demanded. Curly Blazer nodded proudly.

31

'Sure enough, little lady. We are the Slash K ranch's top hands and we do whatever Mr Groff Potter says on account he is the man with the big dollars. Sad to say, you are at the no-lucker end of the scale. If Mr Potter tells us boys get rid of the nesters, get rid of you is what we do.'

'You mean, you kill women and children, don't you?'

Blazer scowled.

'Where'd you hear that?'

'What does it matter? I know innocent people have lost their lives out here; we have heard all about it. I guess your employer is responsible for some of it.'

Blazer removed his hat and scratched his head with a frown.

'You heard stuff like that, yet you still kept coming in your rickety old rig – just two dames and a yeller-belly? Why, you might be right pretty but that sure sounds dumb to me.' His manner turned hard again. 'Well, you turning about or ain't you?'

'No, we are not.'

'Emma,' Jasmine cried from the Conestoga. 'For heaven's sake, don't antagonize them!'

'An-tag-onize,' Blazer said slowly. 'Good word.'

Then suddenly his gun came up and he

cocked it with a threatening click.

'OK, enough jawbone. Turn about or get ready to hurt. What's it to be, nesters?'

Time seemed to slow down as Blazer raised his piece to eye level and squinted along the barrel at Judd. At his side, Dock Ollinger curled back the hammer of his Colt with a click that sounded ominously loud.

They'd said they would shoot; they looked ready to do just that.

'For the love of heaven!' Judd burst out. 'Don't take any notice of her. We'll do what you say – ain't that right, Jas?'

'Of course!' came the frightened voice from the wagon. 'Emma, nothing is worth dying for – for pity's sake.'

A stubborn Emma was about to speak again but gangling Dock got in first.

'Hey, Curly?' he said, twisting in the saddle. 'Did you hear something in back of us just then?'

'No I didn't. Know why? On account there ain't nothing there. So don't start in getting jittery just when things are getting interesting, here.' The cruelty hidden in Blazer's eyes was showing more sharply now. He licked his lips and shook his head in mock sympathy. 'Such good-looking women just craving to die ... sure don't seem right somehow...'

The man was ready to kill. All three saw it now. For all his youthful boyishness, Blazer was a born killer, spawn of a killer clan. He was eager to spill blood, and had already decided that the defiant Emma would be first to die, as his gun lifted again. For her manner told him she was every inch a lady, one of that kind that would never give a wild young gunpacker like him the time of day.

Emma stood horrified now, but would not beg. In her eyes, this entire scene suddenly held a knife-edged clarity unlike anything she had ever experienced: the small fire with the dancing flames, the big sweat-stained horses, that tall cowboy with his unlit cigarette and ready gun, the younger man with his polka-dot shirt. And the naked guns ... and merciless eyes.

She was momentarily acutely conscious of the stars and the smell of the sage and the wind in the treetops and every sight and smell and sound of a life that was but seconds away from ending.

She started as Blazer's gun exploded without further warning and death seared past her face.

In the same instant she glimpsed something startling, inexplicable. In back of the guntoting cowboys, from a deep patch of darkness, a fierce red flower appeared to blossom magically, thinning as it lanced towards the unsuspecting figure of Curly Blazer who was training his smoking sixgun squarely on her breast.

Next instant the deep-throated bellow of the Colt .45 reached her ears and Curly Blazer was punched out the saddle and over the horse's head by the terrible force slamming between the shoulder-blades.

The pistol spilled from the man's hand as he crashed to ground, the fading reverberations of the shot the last sound he would ever hear as his horse stormed away.

Three fast shots thundered. It was Dock Ollinger, hipping around in his saddle and triggering wildly into the gloom. But the invisible gun gave tongue a second time and the gangling rider was hammered from his saddle as though swatted by a giant's fist.

Already the riderless horses were plunging away in blind panic, the sound of hoofs quickly engulfed by the darkness as disturbed birds burst into the night sky.

Emma sank weakly to the ground, her cousin rushing to her side.

'Good God, Emma, what happened?' Judd Steever was too dazed to comprehend anything for the moment. The man had counted

35

himself dead, yet here he was unscathed with two bloodied corpses staring up at nothing from out of the long grass.

Emma knew she was having a nightmare. True, she had seen the gunflashes and falling bodies, yet still could not really comprehend what had happened. Surely living men could not perish so fast or lie so still?

Jasmine came rushing across from the wagon through wisps of gunsmoke, then halted with one hand flying to her mouth as a ghostly figure emerged from the dark of the hollow – a tall man in a black shirt who halted just beyond the rim of the fireglow.

'Were there only two of them?' His voice was deep and steady.

Judd somehow found his voice. 'Yeah ... yeah, that's all, mister...'

The stranger came forward, thumbing fresh shells into a big gleaming Colt. Tall and wide-shouldered, he appeared calm – far too calm considering the violent circumstances, it would seem. He stopped at the fire and Emma Green felt an almost physical impact from the grey eyes that fixed directly upon her.

'Are you all right?'

She had no notion who he was, where he had come from, or why he had risked his life to save theirs. She wanted to be strong yet felt almost ready to faint with relief as he extended a hand to draw her erect. She could scarcely believe that any person could kill with such merciless efficiency, yet remain so calm.

She had never felt further from Salt Lake City than at that moment.

CHAPTER 3

KING OF SLASH K

Most days the Slash K headquarters were near deserted by around nine, save for the house and yard staff and Groff Potter attending his bookwork in his office.

Today was different.

Nine o'clock had come and gone with scarcely a tap of work done. Cowboys gathered in bunches, smoking and talking with grim faces, frequently glancing up towards the ranch house where Potter was visible now, standing on the porch talking with the hands who'd come in with the corpses of Curly Blazer and Dock Ollinger slung across their ponies overnight.

The yard was long and wide, yet even so the riders furthest from the house could hear pretty much all that was being said, mainly because Groff Potter was more shouting than simply talking.

There were three up there on the ranch house gallery with Potter: Cleve Baines, Tom French and Coe Bloodworth. It was French and Baines who'd come upon the bodies after backtracking the horses that had returned to the spread with empty saddles overnight. The pair were regular cowhands, but Bloodworth was the top gunhand on the spread.

'Are you dead sure you never sent them boys out looking for trouble along the river last night, Bloodworth?' Potter demanded, not for the first time. He was still loud, but less so than before.

Coe Bloodworth shook his head casually. 'No chance, boss man.'

Bloodworth looked the part. Thirty years of age and built on outsized lines with a powerful face and piercing eyes, the gunslinger was far less affected by the loss of two hands than was his boss. He'd often remarked that Curly's hot temper, his vaunted notions of his own abilities and his natural recklessness must surely bring him down one day.

So it had turned out. Sure, it was bad for the outfit to lose a top hand and a shooter like Curly, but Bloodworth still didn't believe it rated this long and windy post mortem.

Irritated by his gunslinger's insouciance, long and lanky Potter returned his attention to Baines and Finch.

'So, damnit – tell me again what you made of the sign out there,' he ordered.

'Well, far as we could tell, boss,' supplied cross-eyed Cleve Baines, 'there was a feller and two women camped out there a hundred yards off the trail and close by the river. Tracks say they come by Conestoga. The sign also showed plain enough that Curly and Dock came riding along to the camp, wasn't there very long judging by the sign, when some geezer must've come up on them from behind and blown the living bejasus out of them. Bam! Bam! Just like that. Damndest thing... I mean for top shooters like them boys to be done so easy.'

'Did you track that wagon into town?' Potter wanted to know.

'Well, heck no, boss,' Tom French replied. 'We was pretty shook up – I mean, coming on Curly and Dock that way. And then we also reckoned you'd want to know what happened right away.'

Potter knew they'd done the right thing in reporting back immediately. But at the same time he was desperate for names and information. He wanted that man who'd done the shooting, already had a picture of him forming in his mind.

A pro. He'd have to be. Curly Blazer had been one of the slickest guntippers he'd ever hired and he'd paid him big dollars to perform exactly the kind of duties that had taken the two to the river last night to be blasted into hell without a howdy-do.

He turned away, raised his hands and let them drop.

'Then we have no idea who done my brave boys in,' he lamented. He folded his arms tightly across his scrawny chest and stared fixedly at nothing. He was a beanpole with an outsized head and a face of unusual ugliness and strength. He was the biggest rancher in Calico Valley, a squatter like every other rancher who'd taken up tracts of virgin land before the government officially opened up the valley under the provisions of the Homestead Act a year previously.

There'd been several official attempts to regularize the position of the entrenched ranchers, but when officialdom realized what it was up against in Potter's Cattle Combine, their status quo was accepted unofficially, with only newcomers being subject to the provisions of the Act.

When Potter came to Calico Valley a decade earlier, it had been wild and Indian-infested country, not running so much as a single cow. Today it ran thousands and Potter and his ilk regarded the entire region as theirs by right and were fiercely resentful of the johnny-come-latelys trying to get a foothold amongst them now.

'There's always ways of finding things out, boss,' Coe Bloodworth reminded his employer. 'If it was nesters that done Curly and Dock in then sooner or later we'll know who it was.'

Groff Potter made a negative gesture. He acted aggrieved about the loss of two hands, but in truth could scarcely give a damn, apart from the fact that the deaths had left him short-handed.

He was a practical and ruthless man of affairs who would not have lasted a month in more civilized regions further east. He'd made his own laws for too long out here and fiercely resented the presence of a new sheriff and a law office in 'his' town now.

Bloodworth lighted a cigarette and eyed

41

his employer.

'You fixing to do anything about Curly and Dock, boss? I mean, like today?'

Groff Potter scowled as he stared across the yard. He hated to see men loafing about, but in this instance, he understood. Bloodworth had ordered the cowboys to stay close should Potter have something in mind – like sending them all into town to raise hell and maybe track down the bastard who'd done for his boys.

Potter was tempted. But he was a practical man. For in just a few nights' time the Slash K and a dozen other ranchers planned to combine in a huge raid upon the nester settlement along Indian Flats on the far side of Chad City. Enraged as he might be about the loss of two top gunhands, Potter rated the planned attack as of far more importance.

'Get them out to work and then come back to the house and see me,' he suddenly barked at Bloodworth. Without waiting for a response he wheeled away to enter the library where he immediately poured himself a double brandy.

A pretty maid entered hesitantly. 'Do you require anything, Mr Potter?'

'Yeah. I require you to get the hell out!'

He actually grinned as the pale-faced girl

disappeared. He could still derive pleasure from authority even after all these years of power.

Seated behind his vast desk, he grew introspective again.

It was sometimes still difficult for Groff Potter to believe that everything he could see from his huge windows – this vast kingdom of men and beeves, all that green grass, power and wealth that he had personally wrenched from the wilderness – could suddenly seem to be under threat.

In the past the government had been only too happy to have men of his rugged calibre come in and open up the dangerous regions in the early days. But now that civilization was driving westward they were being labelled squatters and land-grabbers, dinosaurs from prehistory! Today, a man didn't have to battle wild Indians and lose friends and family to the savage land in order to claim a piece of dirt, as he had once done. Nowadays the government was signing pieces of paper and giving away quarter-sections of land, not to cattlemen but to farmers!

Farmers!

Groff Potter's stare darkened and his big nose wrinkled at the very word.

Fences and sheep and truck gardens ... alfalfa fields, for God's sake!

They were as bad as the redskins had been back in the days when they had been a deadly menace – all those dowdy women and half-starved brats cluttering up the landscape where once a man could ride free and far in any direction he chose without even encountering a fence!

He was still seated there brooding when Bloodworth returned some time later. The gunfighter tapped on the door, then strode right in. He was about the only man on the place who could get away with that kind of familiarity. The man was arrogant, powerful and lethal, all qualities Potter required in a lieutenant right now.

'I want you to mount up and go visit the other ranchers and verify they're all ready to go, Saturday night, Coe.'

'Whatever you say, boss.'

'There are one or two like Pecos Doyle and Kelly Rayburn who might come down with an attack of yellow fever before Saturday. Just make it clear that if any bastard doesn't turn up I'll take it as a personal insult and he will be dealt with in that light.'

'Got it.'

Potter leaned back and finally managed a

cruel grin.

'We've deliberately gone easy on those land-thieving scum for a couple of weeks. By about now they must be feeling like things are improving and they don't have much to fret about where the Combine is concerned. They should be sitting ducks.'

'Whatever you say, boss,' Bloodworth replied with a grin, belying his commanding presence with chips of flint for eyes. He was always pleased at the prospect of violence and killing. 'That all?'

Groff Potter nodded but as the gunman headed for the door, he snapped his fingers and beckoned him back.

'Just one more thing, come to think of it. Do you know where I can contact Slinger Dunne and tell him about Curly?'

'Last I heard from Curly, Dunne was hiring his guns in Dustbowl, Arizona.'

Potter scribbled down this information and Bloodworth went to the door. He paused.

'You know, from what I know about them two old gun pards, Dunne is going to take it real hard when he hears about Curly.' Bloodworth's usual arrogance was not in evidence at that moment; the man was showing due respect for a superior gunmaster. He frowned at an afterthought. 'Hope Slinger don't hold us responsible.'

'Doubt it.' The cattleman chewed a nail, then picked up a pen. 'But just in case, I'll make it plain what happened in the letter...' The rancher's expression brightened. 'Say, maybe if this brings Dunne out here, I might be able to talk him into signing on for a spell. Could be he'd be only too happy to go after that dirty bastard who shot his best pard.'

'Might, but I doubt it, boss.' Bloodworth had worked for a spell with Slinger Dunne down in Arizona once, and knew exactly what breed he was. 'He's fussy who he works for and ... and kinda hates big rich fellers like you, even when he goes to work for them.'

'Well, there's no harm in asking.' Potter dipped his pen in the inkwell and began to write.

Riding into the town that night, Jack Stallard found Chad City sprawled brooding and quiet beneath a high-wheeling moon, few of its many houses showing lights at this late hour against the backdrop of the Black Cliffs. Only a couple of the larger saloons and the jailhouse showed lights; he sighted several great wagons similar to the Steevers' Conestoga parked along the wide and hoof-churned main stem.

He stepped down at a saloon hitch rail, tied up the horse and pushed through the swinging doors.

A dozen drinkers and a red-faced bartender glanced his way, then stiffened.

Stallard paid no attention to their reaction, understanding the reason for it.

Naturally the Steevers and Emma Green would have described the 'gunman' responsible for saving their lives, he reasoned. They had done a good job of it, judging by the reactions he was getting.

He walked to the bar and bought whiskey, downed it at a gulp. Standing there with his back to the room waiting for the liquor to bite while the wary bartender refilled his glass, he glanced at his image in the mirror. He was not the least surprised to see that he showed no change.

He never did.

He could put a man in his grave at eight, sit down to steak and eggs at nine. No indigestion; no conscience.

His smile was bitter.

That was how life could harden a man. The kind of life he'd led could either kill you or turn you into a Jack Stallard. No weakness, no emotion, guilt or pain.

He was what destiny had made him, and

two more added to his list made no never-mind whatsoever.

He turned at last to the starers and raised his glass. 'I give you the gun!' he toasted mockingly, just to shock them. And drank deep, knowing that by tomorrow he would be over it. You always recovered quickly from a shoot-out, if you happened to be Jack Stallard. Ever since his first – and most unforgettable kill – nothing could ever touch him again.

That was at once his secret and his strength.

Chaney Stallard camped on a high crest of Yellow Dog Mountain that night. Two hours of hard climbing had taken him far up the faint high-country trail where the air was growing chill and the wind moaned eerily in the firs and spruce dotting the slopes.

He had been forced to don a grimed heavy-weather jacket, feeling the cold more acutely following the heat down on the flatlands.

The youthful killer rode well off the trail before he made camp, selecting a protected cave with good graze for the horse close by.

He awarded himself the luxury of a small fire and ate a sparing meal of jerky and pone-bread followed by several mugs of powerful black coffee. He rolled a cigarette, lit it and stretched out to stare up at the cold high stars.

Young Chaney could not have been more different from his older brother, Jack. Where Jack was tall and handsome, Chaney was a scrawny runt with a scarred and red-veined face, his fierce black eyes set viciously wide over a badly broken nose.

The only visible family characteristic he shared with his brother was his long and supple hands, which showed heavily calloused palms from endless hours of practising with the Colts. For, from a remarkably young age, Chaney Stallard had been uncommonly fast with the sixguns and planned to go on practising and improving until he was best of them all – and everybody knew it.

He awoke at first light.

After first attending to the horse he got a fire going and dropped strips of lean beef into a well-worn skillet.

He heated water for coffee and shaving then set to work attending to his rig and readying his mount for the trail.

With breakfast and the fastidious clean-up behind him, he walked some distance from the camp to a grassy hump where he set about practising his clear and draw without shooting, until satisfied a half-hour later. He then oiled his Colts and rubbed them with a polishing cloth until they shone, every action reflecting long habit.

He returned to the cavern and packed his war bag, strapped on the heavy, double-girthed saddle, and rode out.

It was a cold clear morning in the mountains with sunlight sparkling on grass and trees, and bird calls ringing in the thin late-summer air. Occasionally behind him the rider caught glimpses through gaps in the timber of the cultivated flat lands of Sheba County which he'd quit the day before.

The increasing chill as he travelled coincided with the growing sparseness of the timber as the slow horse-miles flowed behind. Rocky outcroppings bordering the old Indian trail cast their shadows, and the horseman now rode slowly and warily, eyes raking ceaselessly over the terrain that might well conceal a hundred Buck Chavezes.

Chaney Stallard had been dogging Buck Chavez's trail for three long weeks now. He wasn't exactly sure what Chavez was supposed to have done in the north, other than that he was now wanted for murder with a $2,000 bounty on his head.

For $2,000 this bounty hunter might have

been talked into gunning down his own mother, if he'd had one.

In the case of his brother, he'd do it for free.

CHAPTER 4

BOOT HILL FOR LOSERS

The lawman and the gunfighter stood side by side in the morning sunlight, looking at the new graves. They didn't speak for a time, having just walked the three blocks to Boot Hill from the law office where they'd discussed the circumstances of the deaths of the two Slash K gunhands. Ranch boss Potter had sent the bodies of the two dead gunnies for burial.

The cemetery was surprisingly well kept, Stallard saw. Typical of Chad City, he thought. This sizeable town which was at the very storm centre of worsening troubles between entrenched cattlemen and the wagoners from back East, who kept on coming despite the high risks here, appeared prosperous and solid, and on the surface at least, well-run and law-abiding.

On the surface...

But when you stood here in the morning sunlight letting your eyes play over rows and rows of graves, many of them of recent origin, any notion of a normal Western town went out the window.

Jack studied the man at his side. Solid-looking, most likely honest, but looking a little frayed around the edges. A good man trying to hold down a job that was plainly too big for him – that was his summation of the peace officer of Chad City.

He was hardly surprised.

For this was very plainly a town teetering on a dangerous edge, with possibly a worn-out and vulnerable man wearing the star. Yet he couldn't complain about the manner in which the sheriff had handled the river shoot-up. Toovey had calmly heard him out following his arrival in the town with a tale of two corpses, checked his account of the shootings with the Steevers and decided that Stallard had no case to answer.

It had helped that the lawman knew both dead men as gun hellions with ugly records, even before they hired out to Slash K. He'd even conceded that Potter had much to answer for, and felt there was a strong whiff of poetic justice in the rancher losing two of his top guns in the one night.

Walking back for the main street, Toovey showed more interest in Stallard than the deceased.

'And what would your business be, Mr Stallard? Just for my records, you understand?'

That was a big question. Most men in Stallard's line of work might have lied, but he didn't see the point.

'I'm a gunfighter,' he stated flatly. 'I hire my gun to people who can't protect themselves.'

He sounded proud. Maybe he was. He wasn't sure any more.

'Ahem, yes, well I guess that scarce comes as a surprise, I suppose...' The sheriff cleared his throat. 'You know, Mr Stallard, just a couple of years ago a gunfighter showing up here would have been a novelty.' He sighed. 'Not any more, of course. But I'm sure you already have an understanding of the violent climate that prevails here?'

They'd reached the main stem. Stallard halted and rested hands on hips, watching the passers-by.

'Well, I sure know those two gunslingers were about to murder three innocent people in cold blood for no other reason than that they simply wanted to come here and settle.' He put a hard stare on the lawman. He nodded. 'Yeah, I reckon I understand your town, Sheriff – all too well.'

With that he walked off leaving the badgeman staring after him and stroking his jaw. 'More trouble,' the man was thinking. 'As if we ain't got enough...'

Stallard was planning on breakfast when he quit the sheriff's company, but by the time he reached the central block he'd decided a drink might suit him better.

The saloon was quiet and filled with shadows as places like this mostly were that early in the day. A puffy-faced bartender poured him a whiskey which he took to a back table, but didn't drink.

Delayed reaction was setting in.

He lived by the gun – but knew that win, lose or draw, you rarely came out of any shoot-out unscathed.

Mostly at such times he tied one on, then got on with it. Yet there were odd occasions, like today, when he might slip into a reflective mood and get to thinking on just what he was and where he might be heading.

It wasn't smart for any man in his profession to think that way; this he knew full well from experience.

His life simply did not bear close analysis. Sure, the gun ruled many parts of the West at the moment. But that was surely a fleeting thing. He calculated that the day of the gun rule might last another five years, ten at tops. So what kind of future was that?

The emergence of the Western gunslinger had come about in the wake of the war and their exploits briefly captured the imagination of the new, raw land. It was the high drama and the ephemeral nature of the fast gun's trade that attracted publicity and even adulation. The gunslingers' exploits were followed avidly and new gun heroes enjoyed their brief hour in the sun until by their mid-twenties they were either burned out or dead. But there were always the young ones coming up through the ranks to challenge the old kings and seize their own days of glory.

Newspapers, dime magazines and rocking-chair critics were unanimous on the notion: live by the gun long enough and you would surely die by it.

And what did even a top gun have to show for it? Money – but what else? A horse, a gun and an endless trail. But no woman to love him. No child's hand in his own to proclaim his immortality.

A life that tallied up to a column of wasted years...

He sat upright.

'Shake out of it, Stallard,' he muttered. 'You can't gripe ... you made the choice...'

Then the inner voice whispered: was that the strict truth?

'No!'

He didn't know he'd spoken aloud until he realized that the bartender and a weary-eyed percentage girl were staring at him curiously from along the long bar.

He stared down at his hands with jaw muscles working, mentally thrusting back the tentacles of past memory. 'No ... that choice was made for me even before I was born. Kill or die...' he defended himself now.

Absently, it seemed, he lightly fingered the scars on his face with his fingertips, which made him momentarily aware of the other marks of cruelty all over his body. They spoke of pain and terror, those physical mementoes of his childhood. A childhood which ended the day he killed his first man at just fifteen years of age. He had been killing ever since.

He took another pull on his drink and felt the past crowding in like a dark tide.

There had always been odd times in his

life when he felt the past beating against him like a shadowy tide which could not be stilled. Times when, instead of merely accepting himself as he was, he felt driven against his will to look back into the dark past at the elements that had shaped and moulded him into what he was today.

Gunfighter. Manhunter. Self-appointed enemy of human scum – such as his father had been. It was the only life that fitted someone who'd known violence and cruelty from the cradle, fighting for everything in life – even for life itself. And in the end, killing just to live.

He shifted uneasily and swigged his liquor. He knew it was unwise for a man of the Colts to hurt too much or think too deeply. So he made an effort to look forward, rather than to where he'd been as he did so often, but to where it all might lead.

The gunslingers had long captured the imagination of a West which now often appeared to feed on their deeds. Some of them stood very tall in the public eye, a few had even shaped the history of the West.

But always the bullet was waiting.

It could come from the rusty old single-shot fired by some drunken dry-gulcher lying in wait, or he might stop the one that mattered most in a dramatic Main Street gun battle against a worthy adversary, cheered on by hundreds.

Yet the end was always the same. Death had claimed most of his breed before they reached twenty-five. If a man was unusually skilled or just plain lucky he might reach thirty before the odds caught up with him and cancelled him out.

Then would come the headlines, the tears both real and those just for show, with, you might hope, a good crowd following your hearse to Boot Hill. And if you were really lucky, eventually a few lines in some history of the Old West.

It was with a small sense of shock that he realized he would turn twenty-seven on the sixth of November next.

Did that mean he was already living on borrowed time? And, if so, what did he *really* have to show for ten years behind the gun, other than a fat billfold and scars to burn? What else?

A life that tallied to a column of empty years...

'Snap out of it, Stallard!' he growled aloud to the mirror above the back bar of the Lucky Deuce. 'You made your choice...'

But was that the truth?

He shook his head. No. Just another gun-slinger's lie. For the one thing he truly believed was that his bloody career had never been his choice but rather his destiny.

Again he massaged his jaw and studied the face with its familiar faded scar-tracings in the dark bar mirror and seemed to hear that familiar voice in his head:

Get over it, gunfighter! No way back now. Too many ghosts, too many dead...

Drinkers started as he shoved his way violently away from the bar and strode out into the misty night to stand tall and solitary against the sickly gleam of a single Rager streetlamp.

He stood breathing hard until Stallard the gunfighter wrenched control from Stallard the thinker – and fool!

He strode off along the walk where every man made way for him. Soon enough, he knew he would be whole again. And believing he would live for ever.

Chaney Stallard's hearing was acute and he could clearly hear the sounds of a rider working his way down towards the ancient Indian village through the trees while he was still a far ways off.

The runty bounty hunter concealed himself in a nest of ancient grey boulders beneath an overhang of straggling skunkweed, and waited, patient as a hostile.

The trail lay empty before him under a thin noon sun as the clip-clop of hoofs grew steadily closer. He focused upon the bend where the rider would appear and his Colt was held shadowed and ready beneath the curve of his body.

The horseman came into sight.

He was a stockily built young man with a good seat in the saddle of a big black gelding. He rode casually yet watchfully with one hand holding the reins, the other resting upon his hip near the gun.

The hidden watcher studied that broad face. Chavez appeared even more strongly Mexican in the flesh than he did on the truebill tucked into Chaney's top pocket. His nose was short, the jawline strong, while beneath a mane of coarse black hair the eyes were watchful and animal-quick.

Surely a dangerous one by any yardstick.

Chaney's finger caressed the trigger. He invariably brought the wanted in dead, never alive. Chavez was a veteran of the owl hoot who today plainly had no intimation of death lurking so close. All Chaney must do now was squeeze trigger to drill a two-ounce chunk of lead into the Mex killer's skull and he would be $1,000 better off.

Money for old rope!

Yet strangely, with the vital seconds clicking by, his piece remained unfired.

For pride and arrogance had just intruded. Had this been a lesser man riding out of the timber, he would be already lying dead in the dirt by this. Trouble was, handsome Chavez had built himself a formidable reputation as a gunfighter and that was the reason he had not already fallen under the bounty hunter's gun.

Stallard believed Chavez had the right to carve at least ten legitimate notches in his gun handle, if he was of a mind.

This surely was someone worth beating fair and square!

He holstered his gun, sprang atop a boulder, and hollered, 'Chavez!'

The rider halted, hunting for the source of the shout until his gaze locked in on the runty figure silhouetted against a brassy mountain sky.

To most, Stallard would have looked like a nothing. But to the eyes of a professional he appeared as dangerous as the plague.

Chavez's right hand blurred as he made the draw of his life.

Yet Chaney Stallard proved the swifter. It was as smooth a draw and clear as he had ever executed as the barrel whipped up to firing level and roared twice, crashing cannon-loud in the sylvan stillness.

A disbelieving Buck Chavez buckled in the saddle. He triggered once into the trees high above Chaney's head, a second time into the earth beneath him as he fell. He was dead before he struck the ground with Chaney's flaming barrel following him down.

The killer could not suppress a swagger as he clambered down and came light-footed across the clearing to inspect his handiwork. Then he hurled his hat high into the air and howled like an Indian savage as he circled around the corpse.

A stranger happening by might think he'd come upon some kind of dangerous madman. He might have been halfway right. For in those minutes, alone and momentarily unaware of the leg wound he'd sustained in a gundown a week earlier, the killer pacing a circle under a high country sun, was, in his fevered mind, counting coup over the corpse of the brother he hated.

Yet as he gradually calmed down sufficiently to fashion a cigarette with fingers that still trembled with excitement, he was clearly aware of the true significance of what had just happened here.

He had just slain one of Mexico's finest and fastest, which proved beyond all doubt he was at last ready for Jack.

He'd recently heard rumours that placed his brother somewhere beyond the high-country frontier Territory right now. The news had excited him, yet still he'd held back, unsure and uncertain.

He believed he'd shown the wisdom and the patience of a holy saint over the years in the way he'd been prepared to wait a seeming eternity while he grew to manhood and developed the deadly skills he knew he must have to stand any chance when he finally faced down his brother, one of the deadliest guns in all the West.

That body bloating in the sun was proof that his hour had come at last.

CHAPTER 5

MANHUNTER

Jack Stallard came striding from the timberline with the reins of the red horse looped over one arm. The past several hours had been spent stopping by at line camps and small spreads across the brooding stone hills west of the town in search of a lead on outlaw Bo Gaunt, the wanted killer he hunted. Having come up empty-handed he was now left with no option but to search the town itself – again.

His quarry had to be here someplace. The last reliable sign the outlaw had left behind indicated this area as his destination, so he'd followed it. Added to that his man-tracker's sixth sense warned him his killer was here someplace ... maybe watching him right at that moment.

Bo Gaunt had a bloody reputation that was well-earned. For this reason the bounty on the killer's head had kept increasing over time. Still nobody could catch him. He'd killed three men who'd tried.

Stallard halted to catch his breath. Sensing his distraction, the horse attempted to butt him off the rocky slope they were standing on. Normally he might have retaliated. The fact that he didn't showed how preoccupied he was with a quarry which had been out-smarting and outrunning him for long weeks now.

But a wearying two hours later found the manhunter back in Chad City, still empty-handed and growing frustrated now.

A change of tactics was plainly called for. He tied up his horse at the Buffalo Street intersection and immediately set about questioning anyone and everyone who wasn't scared off by his reputation.

Almost immediately he struck pay dirt in the unlikely form of Hump Miller, drunk, loafer, unemployed water-carter, and whittler.

'Sure, I seen a feller like you describe out back of the Road to Ruin saloon two or three nights back, Mr Stallard. Drinking straight from the bottle with a couple of them hard-noses offen the Slash K, so he was.'

Stallard remained sceptical. 'Short, big black moustache like a French pimp?'

'Nah, fine moustache. And he was tall

more'n he was wide as I recall...'

Stallard felt his pulse pick up a beat. The killer's trim moustache was both a vanity and a give-away. And he was certainly tall. In addition, the fact that the man whom Miller had seen was drinking in the darkness away from the saloon tallied with how a man would expect an outlaw to act while on the dodge.

Still, he needed to be certain.

'He's got a kind of squeaky voice, as I recall, Miller. You notice how he talked?'

'Sure, I was drunk but not that drunk. No squeaky voice, I'm afeared. Talked natural just like you and me.'

Stallard fingered a five-spot from his shirt-pocket and handed it over.

'You're doing fine, Miller. Er ... I don't reckon you chanced to hear what it was this man was talking about?'

The bum scratched his stubble and screwed up his train-wreck of a face, a study in concentration. He began to shake his head again, but Stallard pressed another note into the grimed paw and enlightenment lit his features instantly.

'You know, could be I recall his asking about the trails running south. Mebbe the fact that I ain't glimpsed him since could mean he followed the directions this geezer gave him. What do you reckon, Mr Stallard?'

But Stallard didn't hear. He was already on his way back to his horse.

Leading Red for the livery he was forced to thread his way through people mounted, afoot and travelling on wheels along the wide street. There was excitement in the air of Chad City and he'd encountered newcomers from neighbouring territories along with travellers and optimists from Wyoming, California, Colorado and places even further afield.

Land was the magic lure that drew the homesteaders, gamblers, dreamers, shopkeepers, cattlemen and artisans from all over.

Government grants of 640 acres apiece to any honest man who filed a claim was the lure, yet three of every four faces he encountered during that two-block walk appeared grim and bitter in contrast to the starry-eyed expectancy of the odd newcomer.

There was a simple explanation for this. The Lands Office was accepting claims but nobody was able to get them filled any longer. The rumour was that the big established cattle-ranchers were scooping up all the new leases, only a handful of which were they occasionally prepared to unload at exorbitant prices.

But the lucky ones who'd come earlier, before the big rush got started, weren't complaining. This enterprising breed opened shops and stores and joints where a man could buy a bottle at midnight or find a friendly woman even later. The town already had more saloons and honky-tonks than a place with double its population, and a combination of liquor, exuberance, bitterness and high-stake gambling only served to fuel Chad City's ever-worsening tensions between the new settlers and the entrenched cattlemen.

Since his arrival Stallard had witnessed violence aplenty between the haves and have-nots at first hand. There were brawls and frequent shoot-outs which the law seemed unable to control or even adequately investigate.

Three hard-bitten rannies fanned out across the plankwalk were coming his way right now. They swaggered closer, saw who it was coming towards them and instantly gave ground.

As he walked on, he heard: 'Son of a bitch thinks he owns the freaking place!' Then, louder: 'You're on our list, Stallard!'

He didn't look back. He was accustomed to this sort of thing wherever he went. He scared hard-cases yet challenged them at the same time. The fear he engendered had given him a certain pride in earlier times, now he just accepted it as what a man of his calling should expect.

He touched hatbrim and nodded to a clutch of matrons standing before a dress-shop, causing one to gasp and flutter a nervous hand to her bosom.

A short distance further on he encountered a bunch of farmers in blue working denim with red faces and optimistic eyes. They stood leaning against a wall watching several tall cattlemen stride by with their big guns buckled low and hatred in their eyes. You could feel the tension. The dimensions of the local Boot Hill told their own stark story of life in Chad City and the county. As a man of the gun, he'd been approached three times thus far, once by a nester and twice by ranchers eager to hire his guns, one at a 'name your own price' fee.

He halted abruptly before a freshly painted shopfront façade on the Warlock Street corner. The new sign read:

CHAD CITY REALTY & LAND DEALERS
PROPS: STEEVER AND GREEN

69

He was impressed, having half-expected Emma Green and Judd and Jasmine Steever to have flagged down the very first eastbound wagon train they could find and head off just as fast as it was possible to get from Chad City, having taken one good look at the place. After selling up the building and five Main Street acres old Uncle Hector had left them, of course.

He glanced at the open doorway a moment, shook his head and turned to move on. They felt they owed him, he knew, but he wasn't in the mood for reminders of that bloody business at Eagle Feather Creek.

Pausing to light up, he considered the two he'd shot that night. He'd subsequently learned Curly Blazer and Dock Ollinger had been rightly feared in the county, even by the law. Saloon talk had it that both gunmen might well have been declared outlaws, or at least arrested and tried on a number of charges, but for their connection with the Slash K.

Groff Potter was the real power here. He had the land, money, big herds and the hired guns. He also held down the office of city mayor. The rancher had been big even prior to the land boom, now was the biggest.

He moved on. A slim figure emerged from the office behind, made to move off in the opposite direction then sighted him and stopped. 'Oh, Mr Stallard!'

It was Emma Green, stunning in a conservative yet stylish Quaker cloth business suit. She smiled brightly when he turned.

Reluctantly he removed his hat and waited for her to cross to him. He believed any lady as smart as she would have checked up on him by this, would realize she couldn't possibly associate with his type even if he had saved their lives.

Yet her smile seemed genuine. 'Why, Mr Stallard, I had no idea you were back in town.'

'You knew I was away?' This puzzled him. Why should she know?

'Of course I did,' was all she said, turning to glance back at the shop-front. 'Well, don't keep me in suspense. What do you think?'

'About what?'

His manner was remote. It mostly was with anybody who appeared even halfway friendly. He had long been armoured against the world.

'The renovations, of course. You saw the condition Uncle Hector's property was in the day we arrived ... but look at it now. You must be impressed?'

If he was, it didn't show. She didn't seem to notice his distant manner, and next thing she was tugging him by the sleeve and insisting he come make a tour of inspection and give his honest opinion.

The following half-hour passed quickly and pleasantly, he had to concede. But by the time she insisted she must treat him a drink 'to celebrate', he'd about had enough.

He was aware that he'd enjoyed her company. But experience had taught him that while saloon-girls and such like often found his breed exciting, most women of class were repulsed. And Emma Green exuded class.

Yet they subsequently occupied a back table in the almost classy San Antonio saloon for almost two hours.

Not that this meant anything, he thought, reaching for his hat. He'd been down that road before. It could only ever end one way. Oil and water would never mix.

He was surprised when she reached out to detain him. 'Oh, you're not leaving, are you?'

He frowned.

She let his wrist drop immediately. 'Oh, I'm sorry. I'm being pushy, aren't I? Back home folks were always claiming I'm too forward and–'

'Look,' he said with sudden impatience. 'You don't have to go through all this with me, girl. I didn't do anything special for you folks. I'd have done it for anybody. Any man would. But it finished there. You're a lady and I'm a gunman. Those breeds never did mix and never will. End of story.'

He wanted to shock her. She paled, yet her eyes searched his face intently. Then she swallowed and said quietly, 'If you weren't – what it was you just said – the three of us would be in our graves right now.'

'Well, I've been thanked for that ... and that's it. Isn't that plain enough?'

'No.'

'What?'

'I don't find you scary, and I don't take the slightest bit of notice of all that rubbish about how bad you are. I do think you're possibly arrogant with chips on both shoulders, if you must know the truth. Now if you'll excuse me, I shan't burden you with my boring company any longer ... they'll be missing me at the off–'

She broke off as his fingers closed around her wrist, preventing her from rising. For a moment Emma Green found herself staring into the steely blue eyes of a gunfighter, cold and chilling. But then perplexity furrowed

Stallard's faintly scarred features and she heard him say, 'Look me in the eye and tell me my profession doesn't sicken you.'

'What if I responded by saying I find you very handsome?' she asked boldly.

His scowl held for almost half a minute. She didn't flinch before his stare. Then, unaccountably, he found himself smiling as he realized he was being boorish.

He drew her to her feet.

'OK, I know that's a lie,' he said. 'But I mean it when I say you are attractive.'

She slipped her arm through his and guided him for the batwings.

'I love compliments ... even when I have to fish for them. Come on, I think it's high time we newcomers to this bad but exciting town took a long stroll around it, don't you, Jack? I can call you that, can't I?'

'It's my name.'

'We're on our way.'

She slipped her arm through his and laughed softly as walkers made way for them with many turning to stare after them with puzzled eyes.

'What a handsome couple!' a silver-haired gent commented to the lady on his arm. 'A very odd couple, I should say, but quite striking.'

That seemed to be the general consensus as they continued on. But when they turned out of Front Street to stroll along Freemont, where members of the Cattlemen's Association were taking a drink on the second floor gallery at the conclusion of an emergency meeting, the reaction proved very different.

'Judas Priest! Look at *that!*'

Groff Potter's booming voice commanded the attention of his fellow-ranchers assembled there. Several joined him at the railing to stare down, then glanced uncertainly back at the Slash K boss.

'The immoral cohabiting with the murderous!' Potter said thickly, flushed from liquor and outrage. 'He murders two fine boys and they give him the run of the town, by God. Look at them, will you, just–'

'Better take it easy, boss,' counselled his gun guard.

'Take it easy?' The cattleman threw the contents of his glass down his throat then appeared to recover his composure as he followed the receding figures of the couple with a baleful stare. 'All right – I'll take it easy. But only for so long.'

He swung on the bodyguard. 'When did that gunslinger say he'd be back, Jackson?'

'Some time next week, Mr Potter.'

'And what's his name again? Doone, Donner ... this goddamn memory of mine!'

'Dunne. Slinger Dunne.'

'That's the party – Slinger goddamn Dunne! You hear that, boys? Soon as this man heard some bastard had butchered Curly Blazer, he wired me to say he was on his way. I reckon we all know why, huh?'

Sober heads nodded. The name of Slinger Dunne was notorious both here and throughout the wild border lands to the south. For once that fast gun had ridden for Slash K with close pard Curly Blazer late of Slash K Ranch.

'Boss, this is interesting. But we got more on our plate than Stallard or Dunne right now. Remember?' Jackson winked broadly. 'Tomorrow night?'

Potter slugged down the last of his drink, blinked a moment, then his faltering gaze suddenly sharpened.

'Sure ... Indian Flats,' he muttered, sleeving his mouth. He straightened his shoulders. 'No, by glory, I haven't forgotten a thing, mister. How could I? My idea, wasn't it?'

'You mean the notion to clean out those claim-jumping, land-thieving sons of bitches johnny-come-latelys once and for all, boss

76

man? You're damn right it was your idea.'

The rancher rarely smiled, but did so now as he glanced across at the impressive figure of trigger-man Coe Bloodworth, the gunman who would lead the attack this time tomorrow night.

Bloodworth was entered in the Slash K books as security chief. But his real talent was as a killer.

It was their second meeting in twenty-four hours. Stallard wasn't sure if he'd just chanced to happen by the realty office, or if he'd planned it that way.

By the time they were taking lunch at the Mid-Town Diner, he didn't care which. She was beautiful and acted pleased to see him again. Wasn't that enough?

They chatted through the meal and were sipping their coffee when a squad of hard-bitten riders dusted by. When Emma fell silent to stare after them, Stallard was curious.

'What is it? You know those men?'

'I believe they ride for one of the big combines. I've notice several similar groups like that in town today...'

'So?'

She studied him steadily. 'Have you heard any rumours today, Jack?'

'This is Rumour City,' he said, then sobered when she didn't smile. 'Sounds like you've heard something, Emma?'

She shrugged.

'Not so much rumours but ... but I guess more like a feeling...' She paused to rub her arms. 'There's something in the air today. A couple of times at the office I noticed men speaking quietly in corners, breaking off when I approached ... that sort of thing. It also appears to me that there are more cowboys with guns about, or hadn't you noticed?'

'Why, I guess I had, come to think on it.' He studied the street for a moment, then shrugged. 'But I guess this is going to be an uneasy sort of a town until the fighting over land rights has died down and–'

'How did you come by them, Jack?' she broke in.

He stared. 'Come by what?'

'The scars.'

His face closed over. The criss-cross of old scars faintly visible down one side of his face and encircling his tanned throat had been with him so long he rarely noticed them any more, except when shaving.

'I guess they're not attractive, are they?'

'I don't mean that, Jack.' She smiled. 'In fact I think they help.'

'Huh?'

'I think you might be a little too handsome without them. And we couldn't have that, could we?'

He was flattered. Who would not be? He wanted to change the subject, yet when she continued to stare at him intently he realized that she was expecting him to respond.

He shrugged. 'Not a pretty story.'

'I'm tougher than I look.'

He leaned back and sipped his coffee, memories swirling like smoke, all of them ugly.

'Do the scars have something to do with your becoming a gunslinger, Jack?' she pressed.

He was startled. 'Everything,' he responded. 'But what made you figure that?'

'Instinct, concern ... I'm not sure. But am I right?'

He nodded, gazing into the past. His lips twisted in a humourless smile as he took out his cheroots. 'To tell the truth of it, gunfighting was the family business.'

'I've never heard of anything like that. What sort of–?'

'My father was a killer,' he said almost roughly. 'A wife-beater, a brute ... and a killer.' He touched his cheek. 'He gave me these. I've got them all over, had them by the time I was ten.'

She looked shocked. 'He beat you?'

'I always tried to protect my mother ... and he whipped us both. My kid brother, he and the old man were just alike, and he never touched him. They even looked the same, small, ugly and full of hate. I was fifteen years of age the night my father tried to strangle my mother and I grabbed his Colt and shot out both his eyes and threw him on a fire while he was still dying...'

His words faded. He was back in time, feeling it all again, seeing it through memory's prism. Although ashen with horror, Emma reached out and touched his arm. It brought him slowly back to the here and now.

'That's a terrible story, Jack. Your family...?'

'I left home.' His smile was humourless again. 'I'd been practising secretly with the old man's guns for a couple of years ... always planned to catch him sleeping one night and give him six in the guts...'

He broke off, aware that the past was surging against him like a shadowy tide.

'Anyway, I was good with that gun, got a job right off. Now I'm here ... still with the guns...'

The sounds of the Conestoga creaking by were a timely intervention. Stallard blinked back to the here and now and both turned in their chairs to watch the street in silence. A lumbering prairie schooner of the same vintage as the Steevers' wagon rumbled by the eatery, a screeching dry axle drowning out all competing sounds. The rig was loaded to its limits with furniture, farming-gear and children, the four horses looking as if they'd be lucky to make it out to Indian Flats before dropping from exhaustion.

'That's a terrible story,' the girl said sympathetically, when she could be heard. 'Your brother...?'

'Grew up to be the old man all over. Guess what trade he's in?'

'The same as yours?'

'Give the lady a cigar.'

'Do you ever see him?'

'Last time I saw him was a year ago in Colorado.' Absently he massaged his right upper chest where his brother's bullet had come within inches of claiming his life.

The Stallard Sons had been enemies from birth. Jack hated the father his sibling idolized. Jack inherited his mother's hand-someness while his brother was a replica of the old man – and a natural born killer.

Esaw Stallard would have been proud of the man his second offspring had grown into, he knew. Would have dearly loved to have been there that day in Elko when Chaney drove that .32 rifle slug into his older brother, but would not have liked what followed. Losing blood at an alarming rate Jack had nonetheless half-drowned the other in a horse-trough before they were parted by the law, Jack slumping unconscious and Chaney screaming death threats until a baton smashing into his temple felled him unconscious. When he came to, Jack was gone and their trails had not crossed since. Yet whenever Jack Stallard rode alone or approached a darkened arroyo, alleyway or a halfway camp, he was always doubly alert, just in case the day might come when he would look up and his brother would be there waiting with the gun to avenge their father.

This was some fine family history to burden any young woman with, he thought. But she needed to know. Besides, he had an ulterior motive.

He half-sensed Emma Steever might be attracted to him, and he knew she was too fine to encourage that.

The way he figured, his revelations on the Stallard family history should disillusion her for ever. For the simple truth surely was that the Stallards were no good, never were, and their final chapters must surely be written in gunsmoke.

He truly believed he was doing her a good turn by making her see just who and what he really was.

He rose and she looked up at him in a way that made his heart kick. What in hell was happening here? He shook his head and scooped up his hat.

'Time I was moving,' he said tonelessly.

'Do you have to go?' she said, rising. 'I was hoping I might be able to lure you into dining with us. You see, Judd and Jasmine and I have plans for a late supper at the Blue Heron to celebrate our first week in the business, and seeing none of us would be here to celebrate anything but for you ... well, I just think it would be lovely if you could see your way to c–'

'Sounds fine, but I really do have things to attend to.'

'If you change your mind...'

'Sure. Thanks, anyway.'

He left her and headed for the livery. Restlessness was eating at him for some reason and he needed to ride someplace, anyplace – knew he was ready to quit this town right now and never come back – smartest thing he might ever do.

Yet when he reached the livery it was to discover the horse had a slight ankle swelling, which the stable boss was treating.

'Guess he'd be OK to ride if you really had to, Mr Stallard. But otherwise, I'd rest him overnight at least, mebbe twenty-four hours if I was you.'

That was howcome he found himself back at the Nevada Hotel to bathe, shave and change into fresh gear before heading off to see if he might find where the Steevers were dining tonight. He was just doing this to kill time, he told himself. No other reason.

Homer Strong lifted his Big Fifty rifle upon sighting the figure coming through the trees towards his look-out post, but relaxed when he identified fellow homesteader, Hogie Denver.

'Hogie! What the tarnal are you doing over here? You're supposed to be watching the east side of the camp, damnit!'

Grizzled Denver showed his gapped teeth in a grin in the moonlight as he came propping and panting to a halt. He leaned on his squirrel-gun and fingered his sourdough hat back from his forehead.

'Don't take it all so serious, Homer. You know we're only really playing at soldiers out here. That's a far cry from the real thing, man.'

Strong frowned disapprovingly. If his friend wasn't taking the rumour that they could be attacked here on their holdings in Calico Valley seriously, he certainly was.

'Iffen you ain't going to do your job right, man, why don't you go back to camp and root out somebody who will?'

'Ah, don't be tetchy, man.' Denver dug something from a pocket and held it out. 'Here, have a chaw.'

Strong's features softened and he took the plug from the other's hand, bit into with relish.

They started in talking as old pards do, chewed some more tobacco, got up to keep the circulation going, finally stood side by side overlooking the wagon camp on the banks of the Big House River at Indian Flats.

Moon-shadowed hills rose gracefully to the west, while everyplace else stretched immense flatlands fading into the distances.

'You know,' Denver said suddenly, 'I guess I don't really reckon we're going to have any more trouble from them cattlemen now.'

'What makes you say so?'

'Well, just the time, I guess. Since them gunners off Slash K took pot-shots at the Flats that night, trying to scare us into leaving, we feared they was going to come every night to finish us off and burn our wagons. But that's been quite a spell back now and it seems plain that Jack Stallard shooting up Slash K's top guns the way he done has knocked the stuffing right out of them cattlemen. Sure, there's been a few brawls and one or two snipings, but nothing serious. No, I reckon we're right, that they are getting used to us and have finally realized we only want what's rightly ours.'

'Hmm, could be right ... we might be shying at shadows. Let's hope so. Anyways, I'd best be getting back. And you still keep sharp, old-timer ... just in case.'

'See you, pard.'

Hogue Denver shouldered his antique rifle and went trudging off down the long slope, whistling through his teeth and assuring himself that, come midnight, he intended frying himself a slab of that buffalo that Dad Matthews had brought down the day before out on the west flats.

Seemed he could almost taste that steak already as he emerged from a clump of saplings and headed for his position on the south-eastern fringe of the sprawling camp.

The last thought in his mind was that he might make a perfect target there in the flooding moonlight should somebody be lurking in the timber with a Winchester. Somebody was.

The deep-throated roar of the rifle snapped Homer Strong into instant alertness 200 yards distant, but Hogue Denver heard nothing. There was just the terrible blow, the sensation of something exploding inside his head, then nothing but the blackness of eternity as he tumbled forward and rolled down the slope still clutching his old rifle.

That single rifle shot was the signal for thirty armed horsemen to erupt from the timberline where they had been secreted since before moonrise.

Howling like wild Indians they burst from the trees in a storm of pounding hoofs and snarling guns with the cattle kings of Calico Valley, Groff Potter, Nate Lincoln and Brick Rutherford leading the charge.

A look-out on Birch Hill managed to squeeze off several shots before the living flood engulfed him. Shot through and through, the grizzled old Nebraskan went down rolling to be hammered under by steel-shod hoofs as the cowboy army swept heedlessly over his body and stormed on for the wagon camp below.

The period that followed was given over to blood, death and destruction.

The cattlemen of Calico Valley were accustomed to killing. In the early days they'd had to kill Indians to hold on to their land, then found a new need for slaughter against the rustling gangs who harassed them for years on end.

Then came the outlaws, and over time the land barons grew more and more adept at setting up ambushes and staging retaliatory raids against the enemy ... and the graves of good and bad, peaceful and savage, idealistic and primitive dotted the green hillsides and filled the little graveyards on the fringes of the towns.

For several months the conflict between the old and the new had sputtered and flared, often threatening to explode into open warfare yet never quite making it.

Until tonight.

The first cowboy charge that swept around the northern and western flanks of settlers' stockades was costly for the homesteaders, while the treacherous attackers lost but two.

But once the raiders regrouped a mile beyond the camps, then started back with guns blasting, the homesteader fire was increasing in volume and accuracy. Saddles were emptied, horses crashed down screaming, and even as the cattlemen pressed on with their assault they were learning that even the rabbit will fight when cornered.

It lasted for a murderous half-hour.

For a long time following that second charge the battle raged at close quarters, with riders sweeping in and out, firing as they came with retaliatory lead spitting from the Conestogas.

Bullets are no respectors of persons. In that crimson passage of time, the young, the old and the good and the bad all went down, some to rise bloodily to fight on, many never to move again.

Behind the brutal and uneven exchange of the guns, cries of anguish rose until the whole night was madness, confusion, blood and death.

It ended as suddenly as it had begun with Groff Potter's stentorian bellow: 'That'll do them, boys! Let's get out of here!'

As suddenly as it had begun, it was over – with the dark shapes of the horsemen receding swiftly away across the moon-washed flats, heading east and leaving the dazed survivors to stumble from their defensive positions to take stock and count their wounded and dead.

CHAPTER 6

HUNTING MAN

The tracks had been almost obliterated by an overnight shower.

Jack swung down and dropped to one knee, was forced to bend close to the sign in the poor light.

He grimaced. The prints told him very little other than that the horses were well-shod and that at this point the riders had appeared to be swinging away from the south to veer westwards through the lightly timbered country south of the town.

He pushed on. He jammed a cigar between his teeth and bit down hard on it, but didn't light up. Rage still gripped him. No gunfighter could honestly claim to be squeamish, he knew, but what had taken place at Indian

Flats – in particular the death of those children – had hit him hard.

Times like this Stallard felt less a bounty hunter and gunfighter than some kind of natural protector. There had been times in his career when he'd risked his life for other people for no other reason than he knew he must. Times when he'd felt really good about something he'd done, rather than the way he more usually did after shooting down some bloody-handed assassin before he himself might go down.

The sign eventually played out several miles south of the town lights. He reined in and lit up. Back on the Flats, people were still weeping. Deep down, he knew Slash K were responsible. In his mind's eye he pictured their guntippers, tall, well-mounted, arrogant. In particular he envisioned Bloodworth, their top gun, who'd impressed him from the outset as a man to be treated with respect. A natural born killer, if he was any judge.

His jaws tightened. He knew he was working himself up to something, couldn't help it. Assessing the enemy's real strength, he narrowed it down to just three – Bloodworth plus his shadows, Rush Ekron and Connie Clanton. You rarely sighted one without the others, he reflected. He had his own theory about that, which gave him a hint of encouragement. He'd always believed any gun who needed back-ups, no matter how lethal he might be, had a weakness in him somewhere, a lack of total conviction in his own abilities.

Maybe. A man could not always rely on his hunches.

On impulse, the gunfighter turned his horse and headed for the Slash K, not sure what he expected to gain, only sensing it might prove worth the effort.

Fifteen minutes later found him afoot and prowling the fence-line of the ranch's south pastures, the headquarters just a glow of reflected light beyond a long hill a mile distant. He'd already checked the main trail leading in without detecting any significant sign. But a ranch this size had to have more than one entry, he reasoned, and twenty minutes later, he found it.

The gateway was small, not wide enough for a vehicle but plenty spacious enough for riders. The track had been recently churned up by upwards of a dozen horses!

Nothing would convince him that this wasn't proof that Slash K was responsible for the murderous attack at the Flats.

He didn't know how long he remained there, smoking and staring out over the sleeping acres. When he finished his cigarette he took a small notebook and a stub of pencil from a breast pocket and scribbled a note. He wedged it in the gate where it could be easily seen, then turned and headed back for the stand of trees where he'd left the horse.

It was almost noon when Coe Bloodworth rode into Frontier Street with the Slash K gunmen, Rush Ekron and Connie Clanton, trailing behind his big black horse.

The three came clop-hoofing down the dusty main street, upright and arrogant in their saddles, indifferent to the accusing gaze of the homesteaders strung out along the walks.

For, with already another score or more hands from other supporting spreads swaggering about town that day, the Slash K gunners were guaranteed a rowdy welcome to which they responded cockily, reflecting no hint of guilt or regret over the events of the night. The contrary, if anything, was true. As did their masters, the gunmen regarded the settlers as the invaders here, believed strongly that the cattlemen had simply struck back in defence of Calico Valley the night before, as was their perceived right.

The trio of Bloodworth, Ekron and

Clanton had merely been the front line shock troops in that bloody action, although Bloodworth had emerged very much as the top shootist and hero of the attack.

Bloodworth was costing Potter a fortune. The rancher griped about the expense long and loud but nobody had heard one whisper of complaint from him following last night's bloody success.

The Slash K's top triggerman had led from the front in the darkness and chaos of Indian Flats, and no man stood taller amongst the cattle kings today.

Bloodworth was a large man who carried himself with confidence. Heavy-lipped and brute-featured, he was flamboyantly ugly yet carried himself with all the self-assurance of a handsome man.

Glittering rings ornamented his fingers, and flashed in the sunlight as he adjusted the set of his double gun rig. He bent a cold stare upon a ragged bunch of Indian Creek losers gathered outside Doc Noble's, waiting on reports on their wounded.

'You were warned, losers!' His booming voice matched his bulk. 'Learn your lesson and move on – best advice you're going to hear today!'

As they dusted on past the general store, a

homesteader who'd brought an injured son into town earlier, emerged and shook an angry fist.

'You bloody-handed murderers!' he shouted. 'You'll all burn come Judgement Day!'

'You mean it's going to be even hotter then than it is today?' Connie Clanton laughed, wiping imaginary sweat from his brow in an exaggerated gesture.

Bloodworth and Ekron chuckled at Clanton's wit, though Ekron's mirth seemed strained.

Now that they were here on Frontier Street, two of the Slash K's gunslinger trio were beginning to fall prey to some nervousness.

For it'd been Bloodworth's decision alone that they ride in today, a decision prompted solely by the intriguing note he'd received out at the spread from none other than Jack Stallard, inviting him in for a parley.

Groff Potter had warned against his responding and had argued with Bloodworth for some time before finally giving in to his top gun – with reluctance.

Potter claimed to smell a rat but Bloodworth, scanning the message again, read nothing more into it than that Stallard simply wished to see him. They were both, after all, fellow top guns, he'd reasoned. He'd be surprised if Stallard didn't propose a truce, which would elevate Bloodworth no end in the eyes of the Combine, should it come off.

The note that Hump Miller had brought in was short and simple: *Bloodworth, come see me in town and learn something to your advantage. Jack Stallard.*

He saw them as gun brothers, if not right now, then quite possibly so in the future. It simply made sense.

Dust rose sluggishly from the shod hoofs of the walking horses as the trio passed by the City Mercantile and approached the Road to Ruin. A number of men were clustered on the saloon porch, and Bloodworth's bunch searched for a glimpse of Stallard amongst them.

He wasn't there, but they did not know that yet.

An alleyway opened directly opposite the saloon, where Stallard waited in the sharply cut shadows puffing on a slender cheroot. His expression was blank but his eyes tightened fractionally as Potter's top guns came into sight. Yet when he raised the stogie to his lips his hand was rock-steady.

The ranch party had reined in by the time he stepped on the cigar butt. He moved directly along the wheelwright's west wall to emerge from the shadows into the full glare of the street.

Immediately someone gasped, 'Judas – where'd he come from?'

There was a rising murmur of voices and a scraping of boots on warped planking as the Potter guns hipped around in their saddles to see the tall figure coming unhurriedly towards them.

For just a moment the Slash K's killer felt a flicker of alarm. It vanished in an instant and Bloodworth was again his familiar arrogant self as he turned his dapple-grey to face the gunfighter.

'Howdy, Stallard.' His voice was deep and strong. 'Got your note.'

Stallard halted.

'So I figured.' Up close, his eyes appeared cold, maybe as cold as Bloodworth had ever seen. 'I guess that proves folks are right in what they say about you. That you are thicker than a fool as well as being a stinking butcher and child-killer!'

Colour fled from Bloodworth's heavy features as his right hand darted to his .45. In back of him, citizens were beginning to scatter. Ekron and Clanton quickly fanned out on either side of their leader, fingering their gunbutts, hostile yet uncertain.

This was a country mile away from whatever Bloodworth had expected!

Flicking a glance over his shoulder the Slash K gun saw his henchmen in position and looking reassuringly ready to back his play – should it come to that.

Yet despite the thudding of his heart against his ribs, the Slash K's ace still didn't really believe it would.

'What's the score, Stallard?' His massive right paw engulfed the butt of a .45 in a cutaway holster. 'That note you left...?'

'Was an invitation for you to ride in here and be judged for what you did last night!'

The gunman paled visibly. Yet his nerve held as he came to grips with the harsh reality of the situation – and the danger. In that instant he was ready ... as ready as he'd ever been those many other times he'd faced a dangerous man with a gun and walked away from it.

The odds were still three to one, and plainly nobody was rushing to back Stallard's lone play. But maybe the town might be behind Stallard today?

As though in confirmation of that thought, there came a sudden hoarse cry. 'He don't deserve to live, Stallard! He killed my child!'

The sudden roar of support from the mob hit the Slash K guntippers like an icy wave, seeming to come in on them from all sides.

In that instant, Bloodworth sensed Ekron and Clanton both faltering, even though unable to risk snatching a glance at either man. Not with Stallard standing there before him in the deep dust of the street staring up at him with ice in his eyes, he didn't.

Then with a note of genuine grievance in his voice, Bloodworth heard himself say, 'You're nothing but a filthy liar, Stallard. You said if I came to meet you I'd learn something to my advantage. What–?'

'I surely did. And I spoke truly. For I believe it will prove to your everlasting advantage to learn that you are not a man, but a dirty, butchering son-of-a-bitch. It's to any man's advantage to hear the truth about himself. So, either unbuckle that rig or go for your guns, as I will either turn you over to the law or by God I'll shoot you down like the dog you are!'

The shock was all behind Bloodworth now. In the space of a heartbeat, surprise and anger had left him and he was fully restored to that which he had always been – pure killer. His right hand whipped the Peacemaker Colt from its holster.

Even as Jack Stallard came clear, he knew he had never drawn faster. For – with not one but three enemies grabbing for gun iron now – he knew nothing less than his best would be good enough.

The awed onlookers saw the dip of his right shoulder, the starburst of sunlight upon the barrel of his leaping .45, the huge gush of gunsmoke from the muzzle. And blinked in shock as his bullet ripped through the huge gunfighter's gaping mouth and keyholed out the back of his skull in a smoky crimson spatter.

As Bloodworth thudded to ground with his sixgun not even fully clear of the cutaway holster, Stallard dropped low beneath a lancing shot from Rush Ekron and drilled the man through his gun arm to send him toppling over his horse's hindquarters, screaming as he fell.

The smoking gun covered Connie Clanton. But Slash K's number three had seen enough, and snatched his hand off his gunbutt as though it had grown white hot, ducking for cover behind the head of his rearing horse, already blubbering like a woman.

Slowly Stallard came out of his crouch, wreathed in cordite smoke. He stared at the dead man without any hint of triumph, yet with a grim satisfaction. There was no doubting that Bloodworth had killed the nester's child during the raid at Indian Flats. If there really was such a thing as border justice it had just been meted out here.

A hundred silent citizens packing the area came out of their shock slowly as Stallard emptied the spent shells from his revolver and calmly replaced them from his belt. Warily then, just a few edged forward to stare in awe at the huge dead body and marvel at this brutal manifestation of frontier justice, coming so close in the wake of the atrocity at Indian Flats.

Someone cheered, another shouted, 'God protect you, Stallard – you just done what all of us might've if we'd only had the guts and gumption. Let's hear it for Jack Stallard!'

A roar went up but he was already walking away. Yet as the chanting rose and he thrust his way through people who patted his back, he was aware that this was one of the rare times when a gunfighter might have cause to feel good about the trade he followed.

Then the hoarse shout from somewhere: 'Soak it up while you can, Stallard! For Slinger Dunne is surely coming for you!'

The crowd noises faded and heads jerked in all directions, searching in vain for the shouter. For it seemed every citizen knew Slinger Dunne to have been the close pard of Curly Blazer, one of the two Slash K riders cut down by Stallard that night along Eagle Feather Creek.

The watchers scanned Stallard's face for reaction. There was none. He kept walking, and the cheering started up again. He wasn't thinking about Slinger Dunne or anyone else. Only about the rare experience of being hailed a hero rather than a gun killer, something he would savour just as long as it might last. He knew from bitter experience it would not and could not last for long.

He felt like an old man as he trudged off to the law office to tell the sheriff what had happened, and why.

CHAPTER 7

THE CATTLE COMBINE

The three most powerful men in Calico Valley sat around the big round table in Groff Potter's study, the lamplight that flooded over them highlighting both the strengths and weaknesses of their hard faces and casting a flat and yellow gleam across their eyes.

Groff Potter sat in characteristic pose with scrawny shoulders hunched up around his ears, heavy jaw outthrust. A fat cheroot jutted from nicotine-stained teeth and his big bony fingers moved restlessly over the bottle of whiskey standing upon the table before him.

Directly opposite the boss of the Slash K sat Nate Lincoln of the Big Y Ranch. Lincoln was a dude, a tall and angular man with slicked-down hair and a black dash of a moustache which almost concealed his big horse-teeth. He resembled a cathouse pimp yet was a cattleman born and bred.

Forty-five years of age and dying of consumption, Running River ranch boss Brick Rutherford stroked his long handlebar moustache and tried not to cough. His spread adjoining the mighty Slash K was a mere 1,000 acres smaller than Potter's holding, yet was a far inferior outfit due to poor management.

Potter had summoned his fellow cattle kings to his spread tonight following the death of Coe Bloodworth in town earlier that day. The loss of his top gun had hit Groff Potter hard. But he was nothing if not resilient, and by the time he was through cussing out nesters and 'hired guntippers' he was ready to discuss exactly what had occurred and what might be done about it.

'It's got to be the nesters,' he insisted. 'The way I see it, they must have chipped in and put together a poke big enough to hire Stallard to stand against us. That's the only figuring that makes any sense.'

Brick Rutherford coughed.

'That ain't the way I heard it, Groff. My boys tell me the homesteaders was just as taken by surprise by Stallard going up against Bloodworth as we was. And there ain't no talk of any money changing hands, neither.'

'I hear the same thing.' Lincoln sipped his drink fastidiously then dabbed at the corners of his mouth with a silk kerchief tip. The man looked a dude, indeed was a dude through and through. But not soft. Anyone who made that mistake could live to regret it. 'So, what are we to make of it?'

'I still claim I'm right about Stallard,' Potter contended in his characteristically implacable way. 'His kind of shootist don't buy into a ruckus like we've got going here just for the hell of it. They just don't do it.'

'Well, mebbe he is different from the regular run of guntipper, Groff,' suggested Lincoln. 'I mean, what do we really know about this bastard other than that he's handy with a Colt?'

'Damnit, don't you read, man?'

'I can't read,' Lincoln said sourly, wondering whether Potter was maliciously going out of his way to remind him of his illiteracy. The big man was prone to do that sort of thing when his dark moods got the better of him.

'Well, you ain't missing much,' Potter remarked. 'But they had a long piece on the son of a bitch in the paper just yesterday. The same old malarkey you've heard maybe a hundred times. It says he's a pro gun – like we figured. Costs a heap to hire him, they say. Supposed to be unbeatable with the sixguns, which might seem likely after what we saw today. No friends, no home ... nothing but a pair of sixguns and a horse, or so it seems. And of course, he believes he can beat anybody at gunfighting, horse-riding or long-distance spitting!'

'The *Clarion* said that?' Rutherford blinked.

Potter slumped back in his chair. 'Nah, I just added that bit on account that is how the son of a whore acts when he's riding by.'

'Damnit, Groff, that sort of jawbone isn't going to help us along one bit.' Lincoln's tone was sharp. He spread his hands. 'Look, this damned gunman's come here, cut down some of your best hands and made a big man of himself. We decide he's dangerous, agree he's got to go, but he comes out on top again. OK, so it's not the end of the world–'

'Are you making a point, mister?' Potter interjected.

'Damned right I am. And the point is ... we can't afford to let anything change here right now. The nesters are still coming and they're going to end up costing us millions if they get to stay. And unless we get on top again and move the bastards on, like we were doing, Capital City is going to intervene ... and the first thing they'll do is assign a real sheriff here and the Combine will be all through. Can anyone argue with that?'

Two heads shook glumly. 'And so?' Potter challenged. His brow wrinkled suspiciously and he sat upright, eyes flicking from one man to the other. 'Say, you jokers ain't thinking of doing some kind of deal with that gundog, are you? You saying he's got you scared? By Judas, we swore an oath never to rest until we've kicked every last one of those sheep-eaters and thieving plough-walkers clear out of our county. Does that still stand, or doesn't it?'

Both men nodded vigorously. They might

be critical of Potter at times when the big man took risks or overplayed his hand. But basically they were every inch as voracious and bloody-minded as their leader at his worst.

'All damn right!'

Potter flung to his feet, immensely relieved now without showing it. The war against the nesters was not going well, he would admit. And what his henchmen might refer to as 'the Stallard factor', had come from nowhere and was having a damaging impact on the trio's plans insofar as it appeared to be giving the losers and sheep-herders some sort of genuine rallying point.

Potter didn't know for sure whether the gunfighter was aligned with their enemies. It did not signify, even if he was. Their path was clear, regardlesss. That gunshark had to be taken out of the play. Now!

He said as much and two heads bobbed in agreement. Suddenly they were operating in unison again. So a rejuvenated Potter poured fresh shots and they regrouped round the table.

'I want to hear some proposals,' he rumbled. 'You first, Rutherford.'

'Money,' came the quick reply. 'There never was a fast gun who couldn't be bought off.' He hesitated. 'Why are you shaking your head, Groff?'

'Stallard's risking his neck for a bunch of rubes out at the flats,' the big man growled. 'For nothing! That means *dinero* ain't that gundog's Achilles. Lincoln?'

'Well, maybe we could frame him with something like we did with that geezer who was trying to stop us taking over the beef agency,' Lincoln proposed. 'Damnit, you're shaking your head again, Groff. Do you want ideas or don't–'

'Too messy and uncertain,' Potter reasoned. He was silent a moment, looking from one to the other. Then he added quietly, 'I don't just want Stallard dead and out of the picture – eventually, understand? I want him dead and gone now. Killed, buried, fed to the wild dogs. Hear me?'

They heard real good. But they still didn't understand. How did you go about killing somebody who'd just slain your top gun?

'Simple, boys,' Potter stated almost benignly. 'You've got to loosen the purse-strings and hire someone better at killing than Stallard is. Hire him, pay him the big dollars, then sit back and watch Stallard go down like the dog he is. Then it'll be all over bar the burying, and we'll be ready for the next train of homesteaders that shows – ready and waiting!'

'Uh, huh … well, in that case, what about this jawbone we hear about Slinger Dunne? He is rumoured to be on his way back to the county to even accounts with Stallard over Curly Blazer,' Rutherford said after a silence, tossing off three fingers of straight rye. He belched and massaged his chest. 'I mean, if that's true then that could be our break. I don't have to remind you what one hell of a gunfighter Dunne was – is. Twice as quick as Bloodworth to my way of thinking.'

'One gunfighter against another gunfighter!' Lincoln snorted dismissively. 'Only a fifty-fifty chance of putting Stallard in the ground, if that good, although I will allow Dunne's got to about the finest natural gun talent I ever clapped eyes on. And I guess he's going to have his blood well and truly up against Stallard for doing for his old pard, but–'

'We want something sure!' Potter barked, hurling himself erect with a great display of violent energy. 'I was on the streets this morning and they're putting pictures of Stallard in store windows, like he's God Almighty of a sudden. Judas! Let me remind you that right after the raid on Indian Flats we were riding high, and about a dozen wagons had upped and gone from the Flats by midday next day. Now I hear they are turning round and coming back – all because of Stallard–'

'Gaunt!' Lincoln broke in, also getting to his feet. 'That's gotta be the answer, gentlemen. Everyone knows Stallard's staked his reputation on hauling that outlaw back to the judge in Reno ... where they've posted one thousand dollars on his head on account he shot the governor up there! If we could hand him Bo Gaunt on a platter, why, the bounty man would have no option but to go escort him back up north on account that's his job. That'd leave us back in the box seat again instead of sitting here killing nothing but this lousy whiskey!'

Potter and Rutherford stared at him woodenly. Surely this was clutching at straws? If a veteran manhunter like Stallard couldn't run down Bo Gaunt, what chance would they have?

Besides, where might you look for a killer smart enough to have shaken Stallard off his scent?

'I could send out a dozen good men to track Gaunt down and...' Potter began vigorously, then collapsed mid sentence under their stares. They were right, he realized. An unworkable notion. He must be slipping. He was not accustomed to being anything less than totally on top of the game.

So Gaunt was forgotten and they began searching for ideas again.

The debate that ensued carried on far into the night. Potter kept coming up with fresh, ideas, but he was still clutching at more straws and his henchmen rightly overrode him each time.

Either too risky, too expensive, or too dumb. That was their attitude from the outset and this was still the case when the meeting broke off just as dawn touched its grey fingers to the rooftops of the town beyond this big, smoke-filled room.

Fuming with rage and frustration by this, an overstressed Groff Potter promptly declared their triumvirate abolished forthwith. Done and dusted. Told them they both were free to go straight to hell, and then – bitter and sarcastic in his cups – announced that he even might consider selling up and moving on someplace to avoid being here when the nesters took over completely.

But by the time he'd woken from a ten-hour sleep and shaken off his hangover, the county's dominant figure had changed his mind. Again. This came after one of his working girls read his palm and insisted something unexpected was about to turn up that would see his enemies banished and power and prosperity his to command again.

He claimed to believe this gobbledegook simply because he wanted to. He acted buoyant in company, yet when alone was morbidly convinced his great days as leader and power-broker might all be behind him.

That was one full and depressing week for the cattle baron before the man named Slinger Dunne rode into town.

CHAPTER 8

WHERE GUNHAWKS ROOST

Outlaw Bo Gaunt was sipping his third whiskey that night in the high hills at Stockton's bar, Buffalo Hump, the most remote outpost of 'civilization' in fifty miles; population sixty-seven – or roughly thereabouts.

Stockton's was the only saloon in mile-high Buffalo Hump where Bo Gaunt had been holed up for over a week now. That flash outlaw with the big bounty on his head had shown up out of nowhere one rainy night on a horse that could not travel another mile, the rider himself spent and haggard, ground down by illness, long weeks of desperate flight, hunger and privation. And lashed by fear of a man-hunter who simply wouldn't quit.

Fear had rarely troubled this man before. In truth, many who knew him would rate him utterly fearless, which indeed he might well have been – before Kansas City.

'Ahh!' he sighed reflectively now as the raw spirits trickled down his throat. 'They were the days!'

He had good cause to sound nostalgic, for he'd chanced to come to K.C. at the height of its golden period of fame, prosperity and wild notoriety. A deadly two-gunner who could project a boyish charm when not shooting people or robbing stages, Gaunt slotted into Kansas City's big booming life-style as though he were tailor-made for it.

Soon he was playing high-stake poker-games at the Cheviots, where Wild Bill sat in occasionally, went buffalo hunting out on the endless great plains of Kansas with bums and gunslingers, or escorted to the opera the rich tourists from the East whose wives and daughters invariably found him handsome and exciting enough to want to get to know him better.

Many did so, while husband, father or brother were either unaware of what was going on or simply too scared to take up the matter with dashing but lethal Bo.

He consistently won at cards, was on first-name terms with every big-wig and celebrity in town and for that one golden summer he had never ridden higher or with greater style.

Then it happened.

He didn't realize the new gambler at the Lucky Deuce had a reputation as both cardsharp and knife-artist in other places the day he sat down at that table, intent on separating big-spending Kirk Olwood from his last red cent.

Trouble was, that six months he'd spent dodging the posses in the hills of Wyoming with his bunch prior to fleeing to K.C. had left Gaunt a little clumsy and obvious when it came to dealing from the bottom of a deck. When Olwood caught him cheating he reacted the only way a serious gambler would. He whipped out a revolver and was about to shoot at close range when Gaunt fired his little two-shot derringer from between his knees, the bullet ripping upwards through the table top to embed itself in Kirk

Olwood's left chest, the side his heart was on.

Gaunt was long gone by the time an outraged city marshal had whistled up a posse. They never saw which way he went, yet it had been a sobering experience. Unlucky also, as events unfolded. With the intention of getting cashed up, Gaunt travelled south to prey on the wagon trains rolling in by the score, and was doing fine and feeling cocky when a jeweller he was robbing pulled a sneak gun and Gaunt shot him dead.

Turned out the jeweller had influential friends in the capital. Next thing, a huge bounty was placed on his head and it became a straight-out case of run or die. He proved himself skilful and capable in eluding a number of bounty hunters, Rangers and straight-out killers and had continued to do so successfully for weeks on end before he somehow picked up a shadow named Jack Stallard already hunting him for shooting that governor and strangling that woman who wouldn't stop screaming.

That was when the nightmare began.

A dozen times Gaunt was certain he'd given his shadow the slip. Yet sooner or later the time would come when he'd be confidently riding along some sunny trail or another, then glance back to sight a tiny cloud of hoof-lifted dust sticking like a burr to the horizon far behind.

Bo Gaunt was no coward but was beginning to come apart at the seams, when fate intervened. He was ill, exhausted and holed up in the hills of McCoy County when news from Chad City reached his ears. There had been deadly gunplay in that boom town, this story followed up in time by snippets filtering through concerning a major gun battle down there in which Jack Stallard was credited with backing a bunch of ragged-ass nesters against the big cattle combine.

Although sick as a dog from unwisely drinking brackish water during his pell-mell flight across vast Calico Valley, a weakened and shaky Gaunt knew he dare not tarry here so close to Chad City. Somehow he managed to claw his way astride his horse and headed off into the high country where his destination was Buffalo Hump.

The town was just an ugly blink of a place perched on a broken-backed ridge atop the windblown Hardluck Hills, fifty steep miles from Chad City and 2,000 feet above the rangeland plains.

Newcomers rarely came to Buffalo Hump. And no man ever stayed on here unless maybe he was running from the law, or planned on drinking himself to death with all the other losers.

The Hump, as many called it, was no health resort, nor even a halfways decent hideaway for the bums, outlaws, derelicts and walking wounded who called it home, for that matter.

But it was one long and brutal ride up from the plains and it was this aspect of the slummer that appealed most to those with no place else to go.

It comprised one ramshackle saloon, a livery stable, three barns, eleven weather-beaten dwellings and one rickety hotel. Put them all together with a chilly 2,000 foot climate – that was Buffalo Hump.

But every place has its reason for being, and The Hump's was its remoteness. Should a man need to be alone and far from any place, for any reason, Buffalo Hump was for him. There was no trail beyond here and no through traffic that might bring with it such dangers as drifters, curiosity seekers, the simply adventurous – or lawmen.

Naturally it was this last attraction that kept the bullet-holed saloon in business year after year, and continued to attract a certain breed of man, as it had attracted handsome Bo Gaunt.

The long quiet spell up here had done the killer a power of good, and soon he was returned to good health. Meantime, the reassuring news filtering through from the north suggested that Stallard appeared now to be deeply immersed in Chad City's settler troubles ... so why run for cover when there seemed no need?

So he concentrated on polishing up his poker-game and was feeling more robust and cocky by the day. Just last night the busty piano-player had told him she was in love with him, but made him promise he wouldn't pass this news on to her 240-pound husband.

A picture of relaxation, Gaunt was smiling and dealing a hand or two that day when he heard a whiskey-voice further along the long bar say, 'Well, I be damned. Stallard!'

The name went through him like a hot iron. He dropped his hand and whipped out a .45 faster than the eye could follow, was down on one knee behind the table and ready for gunplay – when he stopped and stared. Up front a local boozehound named Clint was shaking hands – not with any six-foot manhunter named Stallard – but rather with an ugly runt in trail-stained rig.

The newcomer turned his head and stared curiously his way as if his sharp black eyes had detected that Gaunt appeared to be acting strangely back there.

Slowly, sweating a freshet, Gaunt uncoiled to full height and concealed his gun behind his back. The ugly newcomer then returned his attention to boozy Clint, affording Gaunt time to bring himself slowly back under control.

He swallowed what was left of his liquor at a gulp then returned his attention to the newcomer with the disturbing name.

The man whom Clint greeted as Stallard was just a runt – certainly no six-footer with wide shoulders and ramrod-erect bearing like his namesake. Nothing like *the* Stallard, that was for sure.

Gaunt began to relax, eventually plucked up nerve enough to make his cautious way towards the front with his right hand a fraction of an inch away from gun handle – just in case.

The closer he drew the less impressive the newcomer appeared, yet another aspect of the man had also changed here at close quarters, and in a way that urged caution.

From a distance in the smoky bar he'd looked the classic loser, apart from those twin guns, that was. But up close you realized with a jolt that the man exuded an almost tangible aura of menace and self-assurance. His eyes, black and staring, swung to fix on badman Gaunt, and sent another chill rippling down his spine.

At that point Clint turned and grinned at him. 'Hey, Bo, meet an old hard-lucker pard of mine. Bo Gaunt, this here is Chaney Stallard.'

Gaunt extended his hand but it went unclaimed. The man who shared the Stallard name barely nodded while studying him suspiciously. This was someone wary of everybody, just as most undoubtedly were of him – or so sharp Bo Gaunt figured.

Chaney Stallard appeared even rougher and wilder-looking than usual today, having spent the past forty-eight hours clawing his way up the southern trackless slopes of the Hardluck Hills through some of the roughest terrain in a hundred miles. There was an easier and longer trail around the hills but by force of habit he avoided well-used trails, which was prudent for anyone with as many enemies as he. So he'd arrived exhausted, spent, and his horse had gone lame, but he didn't give a damn. For this was not so much a journey for him, as a mission.

'Any relation?' Gaunt asked him with an amiable grin.

'What?'

Stallard's voice was deep and powerful. He raked Gaunt up and down with hostile eyes as though finding both the outlaw's style and handsomeness somehow offensive.

'Sorry.' Gaunt smiled. He jerked a thumb over his shoulder in the general direction of the northeast 'I'm talking about that joker who's cutting up rough down at Chad City these days who's got the same handle as you–'

'So!' Chaney cut him off. 'Still there, is he?' He turned to Clint. 'I told you about him last time I was here, didn't I?'

'Sure you did, man. As I recall, there's no love lost 'twixt you Stallard boys? Matter of fact I–'

'I heard he was in that county but feared he might have moved on by the time I got here,' Chaney Stallard interrupted, knuckles standing out whitely as he gripped the bar edge hard. He turned his head to stare at nothing. 'Sure glad that ain't so on account I've come a long way over a heap of years to find him ... yessir, I surely have...'

In that weighty moment, Bo Gaunt glimpsed murder in the depths of glitter-black eyes, and felt a sudden kick of excitement.

'You know, it's a real honour to meet you, Chaney Stallard,' he insisted, producing a fat roll of notes. 'Here, let me buy you a shot. Hell! You too, Clint. You know, I've a hunch that this might be what you could call, well met ... damned if I don't!'

So two deadly guns who both hated Jack Stallard sat down at the same table, and the high country wind moaned softly from the south.

He was a little drunk when he turned in but that didn't prevent him from having the dream.

The dream for Chaney Stallard was always the same. For it recalled the old oft-revisited memories of a far distant time and place that had actually existed when he was half-grown in their old hometown in the south many years earlier now.

His father had been dead for years and his mother was dying from pneumonia, her mind beginning to go. Brother Jack was twenty-three while he was eighteen. They'd gone into the sickroom together to speak with their mother before she left them, yet her face had turned to a mask of horror when she saw Chaney and she'd screamed wildly and ordered Jack to take him out.

'Can't a body even die in peace?' she'd cried. 'Oh get him out, Jack. Get him out of my sight for pity's sake!'

Jack had insisted to him later that, in her delirium, she must have mistaken him for their late father, whom he so closely resembled.

That was how Jack explained it.

But Chaney knew the truth.

His mother had always hated him as fiercely as she'd loved Jack. The brothers had always been distant, one from the other, but it was not until that day that true hate was born. He'd always hated Jack for killing their father, but hated him with a far greater intensity because his mother had loved him so. And Jack, he knew, had always detested him because he so resembled their father.

And he saw in the gallery of his memory that day long before his mother died when his father – who never beat him because they were the same, but who hated Jack because he was so different, took to Jack with the whip again ... and for the last time. The old man was beating Jack to a pulp when his gun slipped from his pocket. In a moment Jack had it in his hand, rammed the barrel into his father's snarling mouth and blew his brains out through the back of his head...

The vision slowly faded and Chaney snapped up to a seated position in his narrow bunk, still fighting off the dregs of the vivid dream, his breath sobbing in his throat. He swung bare feet to the floor and crossed to the open window to stare north ... towards McCoy County and Chad City.

'Four years,' he muttered, his mouth twisting like a knife wound. 'It's taken four years since our mother died to know I can kill you ... brother. But I'm coming for you now ... and I won't be coming alone ... on account I aim to make double sure of you. Four stinking years, but I know the old man will understand why I took so long to square his account...'

Emerging from the back rooms of the Road To Ruin saloon where he'd just finished an early supper, Jack Stallard glanced sharply towards the long bar.

Sure enough, as the waiter had informed, towering Groff Potter dominated the group that had gathered around Slinger Dunne, the new arrival and the big name on everybody's lips in Chad City today.

Potter had his back turned to Stallard at

that moment but Dunne sighted him instantly. Their eyes locked. Neither man blinked or showed emotion. The Slash K party turned sharply, and when they stared in his direction Stallard detected a new brash cockiness about them that had not been present before Dunne hit town.

Potter growled something and they returned their attention to the newcomer. The smiling gunfighter said something that made them all laugh.

Stallard's expression showed no change. The return of the prodigal gun, Dunne, had sent tremors through Chad City and had certainly caused excitement out at the big ranch. Both sheriff and mayor had visited Stallard earlier that day to seek his reaction on the return of the Slash K's former top gun from their range war days. He'd shown no reaction. He believed the day any gunfighter started shying at shadows was the day he should hang up the Colts and take up chicken-ranching.

He hitched at his gunbelt and threaded his way slowly between the tables. The place was doing good business mid-afternoon and whiskey and money flowed freely. Yet just beneath the laughter and hum of voices he detected a hidden pulsebeat of tension. He was conscious of men turning to stare after him before looking away when he gave them the cold eye.

Several drinkers appeared openly surprised to see him still around town. For it was rumoured he'd been camped on the trail of the notorious outlaw Bo Gaunt upon first reaching McCoy County, and with things settled down both here and out at Indian Flats over recent days, many had expected him to go off on that trail again.

He'd considered doing so, yet only briefly. On the surface it might seem the town appeared calm enough after the violence, save for the odd brawl or domestic. It also followed that the longer he remained here the less his chances of catching his killer must be.

Yet he stayed on. And if Stallard himself could not be sure of the reason for this delay, how could others expect to understand?

'Mr Stallard!'

He halted to see a homesteader beckoning from a nearby table. Homer Strong was kinsman of the nester who had lost his daughter in the battle with the Slash K at the river. Tall, gaunt and rugged with a Big Fifty long rifle lying carelessly across his table, the man was nursing a jug of beer yet didn't appear drunk.

Stallard crossed to him. 'What is it?' He felt he sounded like a sheriff. Maybe he even acted like one. He'd never seen himself in that light before Chad City. He'd rarely stayed in any town this long when on a manhunt.

'Them geezers over by the bar, Mr Stallard. The K bunch. They've been gabbing and bragging and carrying on ... and I've been kinda listening in.'

'So?'

The man leaned towards him conspiratorially. 'They's cooking up more trouble ... I'm sure of that. Sounded to me like some want the spread to back Dunne to go against you, then run us poor folks all off when you're dead. But from what I could hear from Potter himself, he seems to reckon they need more than just one gunfighter to prop them up. I reckon that is what they are about – chewing over who they can get to back Dunne's play, and how much it might cost.' He leaned back and spread his hands. 'So I guess our troubles ain't rightly over after all, huh?'

'Maybe so, maybe not,' Stallard said, moving for the batwings. 'Better go easy on that stuff, old-timer.'

'Easy? You bet, Mr Stallard.'

When he glanced back he saw Strong

127

promptly drain his glass at a gulp, and who could blame him?

As the batwings slapped to silence behind the gunfighter's tall form, a sudden silence fell over the ranch party strung out along the long bar. They'd been feigning nonchalance up to that point, yet every Slash K man had been watching covertly to see how returning hero Slinger Dunne might react to his first sight of their common enemy.

Dunne's initial reaction was to a take another swallow of cold beer. This fast gun had strutted in the limelight all his life, and loved it. But his vanity was a strength, not a weakness. He'd seen too many class gunslingers brought low by over-estimating their abilities while minimizing those of others.

He took another sip and fingered his handsome blond moustache. Potter's patience snapped.

'All right, goddamnit, what do you make of him? Is Stallard the real thing or just another phoney, mister?'

'Phoney?' Dunne seemed puzzled by that. 'He cut down two of your top guns at Eagle Feather River, and then Bloodworth. He's pistol-whipped your toughest hands good, and he damn near took the Slash K on by himself after Indian Flats. And you're asking me is he the real thing?'

Potter scowled petulantly. He hated it when people answered one question with another. He'd like to snap back at Dunne but daren't take the risk of falling out with him. For Slinger was his ace in the deck now, the only real top card he was holding since Stallard put Bloodworth in the ground.

'OK, OK,' he said testily. 'I'll put it in plain American. Can you take him out or can't you?'

'Ahh, same old Groff.' Dunne smiled tolerantly. Then suddenly he straightened from the bar and turned serious. 'His rep speaks for itself and he looks the real thing to me. What else do you want to know – boss man?'

Potter scowled. This gunslinger had never shown proper respect before, wasn't doing so now. His breed thought they were the masters of creation – until somebody hanged them or blew them out of their fancy boots!

Then he realized that anger was grabbing hold.

He could not afford that.

He fought for control and achieved it. Then he settled down to study his position calmly. The reality of the situation was that Dunne was here in Chad City and ready to go back on the payroll – he hoped. The man was a gun asset and had the charisma that could attract others to back his play, as he'd done on the spread in the past. He was a hero on the Slash K and they were running short of that breed. So, this cattle baron could afford to swallow his pride. For now.

The Cattle Combine had lost considerable ground over the past week, and Potter must believe one man might turn it all around before he lost all respect and the wolves began to gather. He had no real friends, but he did have power. And he would exercise it.

A vainglorious sense of self surged through him. The county would be his, and it would be without any Conestoga scum and no Lands Office doling out slabs of prime grazing ground to any broken-assed loser who asked for it. He would live to see the Combine ruling the council, the law office, and maybe even the Territorial court before he was done!

'Slow down a tad, Potter,' he muttered under his breath.

Maybe his vision sounded too ambitious to turn into reality? he pondered. And yet, he'd almost had it in his hands just a month ago, and could still remember how great that had felt.

The stark reality of his situation now, was

that when all the hoopla and brag-talk was brushed aside – his future and that of the whole town now hinged on just one man.

Stallard.

Anger gripped him again.

The nesters and the losers had elevated a lousy gunslinger to become their great white hope! It was time he stopped pussy-footing around and found out whether Dunne had what it took to rid him of Jack Stallard, or not.

'OK, OK,' Dunne said as though reading his thoughts as Potter whirled to face him. The gunman had known all along why the cattle baron had sent for him. 'I've seen him, I'm weighing him up, and when I've decided when and how I'll take him down, you'll be first to know.'

Groff Potter's ruthless features sagged in genuine relief. 'Now that's the sort of talk I want to hear!' He smiled broadly. 'And suddenly I've a real powerful feeling you could do that job standing on your head, Slinger boy.' He raised his voice to a shout. 'OK, boys, let's hear it for the Slinger! Hip-hip hooray!'

They were still cheering when the old man with the rifle rose from his table nearby and approached.

'And what are you devils hatching up now?' he shouted angrily, banging his rifle butt on the floorboards 'The death of another child? Or maybe you're planning bigger things now, like burning down an orphanage maybe? You listen to me, Groff Potter, you can't just go on–'

'Damnation!' Potter barked. 'Do I have to put up with this?'

'Leave it to me, boss man,' Slinger Dunne said with that easy smile. 'You want me to earn my keep, so here goes.' He turned. 'Beat it, old-timer.'

With the words he gave the old man a shove. The old man teetered and fell backwards in a tangle of chairs, accompanied by the roars of laughter that boosted Potter and his party out through the swinging doors. They were moving boisterously for their tied-up horses when they realized something was happening further along the street.

Tramping the plankboards, Stallard paused to tug his hatbrim low against the rays of a setting sun.

Momentarily, Chad City almost resembled a regular and prosperous Western town. Kids playing hoop in the alleys, women in shawls and poke-bonnets with

132

wicker baskets bustling from store to store, wheeled and hoofed traffic rolling by.

While he was taking stock the town was looking back at him. He'd scared them at first, now many were eager for him to stay on – even those yet to come to terms with their admiration of a man of his violent profession.

It appeared that only a handful seemed to want him to quit. A strange kind of calm prevailed these days, even though there were many, Stallard included, who sensed the troubles were still far from over. But the optimism had been gaining ground fast, and many were coming to believe genuine peace might be a real possibility – until Slinger Dunne had shown up on Slash K, that was.

This development, carried sobering overtones of menace and danger, and almost everybody had deduced that Potter and henchmen Lincoln and Rutherford had not undergone any real change simply because they'd suffered some reversals, after all. The sudden appearance of a gun of Dunne's calibre meant Slash K and the Combine would likely still prove a major threat to this fragile peace.

Foot and wheeled traffic surged by as Stallard continued on down the centre of the street, where he eventually halted upon finding himself directly across the road from the freshly painted offices of Chad City's newest realty company.

He half-grinned, something he rarely did, and felt himself relax for the first time since sighting Slash K's new pistol.

He knew she was responsible for that, even as he puzzled to find himself walking towards that building. What was he thinking? That he was a normal man capable of striking up normal friendships? That was loco.

He simply did not understand. Men like Dunne he understood on sight; they were like him, and because of that, he could often predict with accuracy what they might do, say or even think.

Emma Green was totally different.

He'd never known anybody quite like her; they'd seemed to strike a rapport from the outset. A normal man might welcome that and even hope it might lead somewhere.

He was not a normal man.

For a moment he was angry because his steps had led him here again, seemingly without any decision by himself. But halting next door to the realtor's he made himself relax, folded his arms and leaned back against a hitch rail. He was tempted to go in, yet knew he wouldn't. Too dangerous.

What if he got to like her – really like her?

He shook his head. There was no answer to that, and his gaze grew remote again.

Time to move on?

Wherever he went there quickly came the time when he knew he'd overstayed. For he was a drifter and loner and that was how it had always been. That harsh fact of life would always see him move on. His early life experiences had shaped him into a particular mould, hard, solitary, and violent. No point denying it. His kind rarely even made friends, much less got to hope for anything deep or close in their lives. He was a rolling stone. The far places would always call and he would answer.

So be it.

Maybe he'd come to mean something to Emma here in Chad City, however small. But she would forget him soon enough, and somewhere down the road there would be someone for her, a man strong, upright and reliable who quite likely might not even own a gun.

'Go home, Stallard,' he muttered, pushing off the railing. 'Go home, have a few drinks and–'

He broke off as the sound of a curse echoed from somewhere close by. He realized that a disturbance had erupted from a building two doors along from the newly painted offices. Men were pushing and shoving and, as he started across the street, he realized that Judd Steever was involved in a fracas with a bunch of cowboys.

Slash K cowboys!

He quickened his pace and mounted the walk just as Judd, blood trickling from a cut lip, was knocked down and a drunken waddy aimed a kick at his head.

The kick never landed. Stallard got there first and dropped the rider cold with a brutal rabbit-punch to the back of the neck. As the man fell his companions came rushing out angrily only to find themselves facing Stallard standing before them with one hand resting on his Colt handle.

'What's this about?' he demanded. 'Come on, I don't have all day!'

Before they could respond, Judd struggled to his feet. 'It's OK, Jack,' he panted, dabbing at his lip. 'I ... was just pasting up a poster advertising blocks for sale out at Indian Flats ... and these men took exception. No real damage done.'

Stallard swung on the bunch again, cold-eyed and dangerous. If others had forgotten the child killed out at Indian Flats a week back, he had not.

'Get your horses!' he ordered.

A beefy redhead cursed. 'What do you mean–?'

'You're leaving town. Pronto!'

Some moved, others did not. A sixgun appeared as if by magic in Stallard's hand and although the redhead threw up meaty arms defensively, the sweeping barrel still crashed through and opened a three-inch gash in his forehead. The blow felled him to the planks like a beef carcass.

'Get him up and get the hell out!' Jack said.

This time there was no tardiness in following orders, and a silent crowd had gathered by the time the Slash K party got mounted and started off.

Someone called his name and Stallard swung to see the sheriff mounting the steps. 'What's going on here, Mr Stallard?'

Stallard explained. The lawman of Chad City scratched his head and appeared highly nervous. Stallard understood why when he sighted the Slash K bunch from the saloon hurrying their way down the centre of the street with wagons and walkers making way for them.

Groff Potter was leading, angry and red-faced.

'Just what in the name of all that's holy is going on here?' he demanded, bounding up on to the porch. 'What happened to my man–' He paused and stared directly at Stallard. 'Or can I guess?'

'Esaw struck this man, Mr Potter,' the sheriff explained. 'I guess Mr Stallard intervened.'

'Assaulted, you mean! By glory, I'm not standing for this, Sheriff. I demand you arrest this ... this backshooter, and I want him charged with–'

'Calm down, sir,' the sheriff said. 'The incident is over and–'

'And you're horning in on something you didn't even see,' Stallard cut in, standing with his back to the wall where he could watch the entire Slash K bunch at once.

His eyes flicked at Dunne then cut back to the rancher.

'You don't run things here any which way you want any longer, Potter. The quicker you realize that the healthier you will be. OK, your boys are moving out, so you bunch can go get your horses and join them.'

The rancher's face was bloodless but his eyes blazed with incandescent anger. Suddenly he whirled and clutched at the sleeve of Slinger Dunne.

'This is it, gunfighter,' he half-choked. 'This is the reason you came back. The trouble ain't those nester scum, it's this nobody, by God and by Judas! Deal with him. Take him out and write your own ticket—'

'Yeah, Dunne.' Stallard's voice was cold and his eyes held a hard shine. 'You came back to be a hero and you'll never have a better chance than now.'

It was a challenge, raw and naked, and it lay at Slinger Dunne's feet.

Dunne was the real deal. He'd earned his reputation honestly and had returned to the county on a big contract to boost the K's gun force in its battle with the nesters.

But this was too rich for his blood, he knew. Stallard was too fired up, too confident. Dunne was not afraid, but neither did he intend being suckered in on another man's call. He would always wait his moment. Timing was all, and this time was simply not right – for him.

'Another time mebbe, Stallard,' he said quietly, then turned on his heel and walked away.

Groff Potter sagged against an upright as though stricken. Around him, Slash K men waited uncertainly, unsure what he wanted of them now.

The sheriff solved that problem. 'Clear this porch!' he barked authoritatively. 'Go on, all of you. And that includes you, Mr Potter. It's over, and I'd appreciate it if you'd take your crew back to the spread and...'

His words faded off as Potter barked an order and went lunging off up the street, his men trailing behind him. Dunne was last to go, deliberately taking his time and glancing back once over one shoulder at Stallard with an eye as cold as death.

When Jack finally turned away it was to see Emma and Jasmine watching from the office two doors down. They had seen it all, he realized, and he wished they hadn't. He caught Emma's eye but her look told him nothing.

He turned and walked off in the opposite direction before turning in at the first saloon.

CHAPTER 9

THE LAST HEROES

By the time Slinger Dunne reached the cross-trails known as the Threeways that night, he was cool again. The blow-up with Potter had been a bad one, and in the end, as usual, that bad-tempered old bastard had gone too far. Sure, he'd acted contrite later after his gunslinger had quit. Too late! For Dunne had had a long and torrid day of it and was in no frame of mind to take any gaff from anybody.

So he was riding out, even while aware he would be back. He had a major score to settle here, and would wager Stallard would be instinctively smart enough to realize he'd come back to front him – on his terms at his own time.

In the meantime he would rest up some and take it easy. He knew just the place.

He selected his trail and reckoned he should reach Buffalo Hump around midnight.

Stallard was seated on the upper balcony of the hotel, boots crossed upon the railing and studying his map carefully, when she suddenly appeared.

Indeed, she appeared so quickly and in silence that he actually grabbed his gunbutt before he could stop himself.

He flushed a little as he came erect.

'Emma,' he said formally. 'Ahh ... I wasn't expecting–'

'Of course you weren't,' she said breezily, pretty and neat in poke-bonnet and crinoline dress. 'Sorry if I startled you...' She broke off when she saw the map. She frowned. 'You're leaving?'

Was it his imagination, or did she sound disappointed?

'Well...' he began, then hesitated. Strange. He was never lost for words with anyone else. Not ever. He cleared his throat.

'Maybe,' he confessed. 'Please, take a seat.'

She remained standing, studying him in that odd and disturbingly direct way she had. 'Were you intending to leave without saying goodbye?'

He had regained his balance now. He went to the railing and perched upon it, one leg swinging.

'Guess I was,' he said honestly.

'That would have been very rude.'

'If you say so,' he said, wondering why she had come, why she seemed almost cross with him now. 'Can I get you something?'

'I need a driver.'

'What?'

She gestured at the street. 'I am visiting the Flats this morning and it's too far for me to travel alone...'

Suddenly he was relieved. He'd feared that yesterday's violence on the streets might have proved one incident too many as far as she was concerned. And indeed he had just been studying a map of the county, trying to figure where Bo Gaunt might have been heading ten days earlier when Stallard had broken off the manhunt.

He was on his feet and reaching for his hat.

'Your carriage awaits, ma'am,' he said, making a rare attempt at lightness.

It drew a smile. 'I knew I could count on you,' she said, and stepping lightly past him, led the way for the stairs.

'Where are you going – pard?'

Bo Gaunt's tone was jocular. There had been plenty of rye whiskey put away that night, and even though his drinking partner at Buffalo Hump's mountain top saloon might be pretty humourless and with few good yarns to tell, handsome Bo had taken to Slinger Dunne like a long-lost brother – and that was even before they'd discovered that both were on the dodge from the same gunfighter, the intimidating Jack Stallard of Chad City.

From the moment they digested this fact of life their friendship was signed and sealed, and they settled down to some serious story-telling – and drinking – until Chaney Stallard suddenly rose and headed for the doors.

'Hey!' Dunne called, perplexed. 'Where you off to, pard?'

'Getting some air,' came the gruff response. 'Line up another two shots while I'm gone.'

Chaney Stallard didn't call him 'pard', had never used that term or any like it to anyone in his life.

The wind at 2000 feet stung his gritty eyes as the killer walked grimly into the face of it and glared off down the rutted trail winding downhill and to the north.

Chad City and the cattle country lay in that direction.

Then he turned and picked out that rough animal pad which led off from the goat-track trail he'd followed up from the low-lands to the south after killing his pursuer some twenty miles distant.

He hadn't known it at the time, but that track had brought him good luck by dumping him at Buffalo Hump where he'd met Bo Gaunt.

He hadn't cared for the looks of that flash bastard. At first. But then scarcely anybody ever impressed him. Now he was prepared to regard him as a henchman – at least for as long it might take to undertake a job of mutual interest in a town to the north.

Chaney Stallard did not believe in coincidence, luck, signs or portents ... none of that kind of bulldust. Yet from time to time he encountered some things that were hard to explain otherwise to his satisfaction.

On meeting up with that slick dude back there, Chaney had sized him up immediately as a class gunslinger, like himself; he might even be a damn good one – exactly like himself. Men of the same trade always had much in common, and the antisocial Stallard had found himself surprisingly ready to discuss such things as old enemies, gunfights and even lawmen they had met with this new acquaintance; he was uncomfortable with the word 'friend'.

145

Then Chaney had got around to asking some questions about his brother, which was when he learned how Jack had hunted Gaunt across a couple of hundred miles before getting delayed for some reason down on the rangeland.

Gaunt was a tad reserved initially. But after Chaney spat out some of his vicious hatred concerning his sibling, the flashy gun-dude opened up until Chaney realized, not surprisingly, he supposed, that they both hated Jack Stallard's guts.

This surely was a coincidence with a kick to it. Stomping along this lousy mountain-top road with the wind blowing its guts out and buffeting him from side to side now, Chaney could not recall which of them had first floated the idea of their joining forces in order to make a dead-set certainty of putting Jack in the ground. But whoever it had been, both instantly saw the hard and unarguable good sense about that proposition.

Each man fiercely believed he could take Jack Stallard out of the game alone when his time came ripe, with Chaney, in particular, hungry not only to do the killing but, in doing so, claim the glory of defeating his brother fair and square.

And yet, as both quickly came to realize as

that long night seemed to flash by on a surge of excitement and a sense of urgency, surely the end was far more important than the means? For it was dimly possible – at least from the intelligent Gaunt's point of view – that just one gun going against Jack Stallard the nonpareil, could well go down.

But never two.

It took hours to persuade Stallard, but in the end success was Gaunt's reward. Half-drunk by then, they at last shook hands and clapped each other on the back to seal the deal, each now rock-solid certain that, however the endgame might be played, the one man who would never walk away from it would be Jack Stallard.

And Chaney was now convinced that some power stronger than themselves had engineered their coming together – for that single purpose.

He kept walking.

The wind buffeted him strongly but he stolidly refused to stagger any. Nobody seeing him out here in the windy darkness could have guessed what passed through his dark brain in that exalting high-country hour. Perhaps he reflected on those he had killed; there had been many.

But it was far more likely that all the evil

that had been nurtured within his twisted and bitter heart was tonight approaching maturation, swelling and enriching him as it approached its fullest flowering.

Suddenly a more violent gust caught him and boosted him back in the direction of the saloon. He did not fight it now, happy to get back to his new flash friend inside.

Gaunt welcomed him back as though he'd been gone hours, the new shots were lined up on the bar, there was a girl singing in back and the creaking of the timbers seemed to have a welcoming sound.

Either that or he was getting drunk.

Not that it mattered. He could still talk, and did.

'Still can't believe the luck,' he said in that deep rough voice. 'Two of us – gunning for the same bastard.' He clinked their glasses. 'Here's to our enemies, may they be dead soon!'

'Dead, buried and forgotten!' toasted Bo Gaunt. 'And soon, of course.'

Chaney drained his glass at a gulp, sleeved his mouth.

'Just think, Stallard's likely walking that main stem down there in that lousy town, chest out, bragging his head off and thinking he's home free and will live for ever. But even if he's lucky, he'll be lucky to see tomorrow night.'

'You bet. I mean, the bastard might be good, but you're good, I'm good, and two of us are going to be odds-on too damned good, hah! hah!'

'To Stallard!' Chaney Stallard toasted, holding his glass high. And both laughed boisterously even though neither was the laughing kind.

The day wore on and they continued to drink and refine their plans. The occasional client came and went, the wind continued to buffet the walls of the jerry-built saloon. Eventually a horseman came in off the north trail and dismounted, allowing the wind to boost him to the closed doors.

He stepped inside and Bo Gaunt turned sharply on his stool. 'Slinger?' he said. 'What...?'

Slinger Dunne stared as he brushed his hat back off his face. 'Bo?' He grinned. 'So, this is where you skedaddled to when Stallard looked like catching up with you?'

He came across quickly to shake hands and was introduced to Chaney, who nodded coldly but made no attempt to shake hands. Indeed he appeared suspicious, but then he suspected everybody.

'What's your trade, Dunne?' he asked bluntly.

'Hey, you don't have to worry none about Slinger here,' Gaunt declared. 'He's a top gunslinger like we are, Chaney. Worked for Slash K for a spell. Tell me, Slinger, what brings you up here to the high lonesome?'

'It's a long story,' said Dunne, signalling for a drink.

'I'd like to hear it.' Stallard's tone was hard. 'I always like to know who I'm drinking with, mister.'

'He's OK...' Gaunt insisted, but Chaney's stare silenced him.

Dunne considered a moment. He was a dangerous man on a short fuse tonight. But he was also weary and peeved, so he took the easy route.

'I had a falling-out with Potter and elected to come up here while I figured my next move.'

'What was the ruckus about, man?' asked Gaunt.

'Well, you know that gunfighter who's got everybody walking on hair down there?' Gaunt and Chaney traded glances, then nodded for Dunne to continue. 'Well, Potter tried to sic me onto him, but the time wasn't right. We fell out ... and here I am.'

'Let me get this straight,' Chaney Stallard said sharply. 'This Potter geezer ... he wanted you to gun Stallard?'

Dunne looked puzzled. 'Yeah, but why are you–?'

'I don't believe it!' Chaney was astonished. The killer almost laughed but had really forgotten how.

'First Gaunt here, then me, now you. Three of us ... and just one of him! Damnit all to hell! Who would believe it but–'

His words cut off and the killer's face underwent a sharp change. He sat staring at his companions, whose expressions were mirroring his own, all three slowly registering the fact that here, in the unlikeliest of places, they were being confronted by something beyond the normal, maybe even something predestined.

In the deepening quiet three brutal men of the gun, each holding hatred in his heart for another, sat marvelling at what had taken place here, and what it might mean.

Once agreeing that blind destiny had thrown them together for a purpose, excitement ran high but it was Chaney Stallard who eventually reined it in.

'OK, this was meant to happen,' he stated

in that rough deep voice, black eyes glittering and unblinking. 'And we can count the bastard dead right now, on account him and Bill Hickok couldn't stand against the three of us.'

'Damn right,' Dunne grinned wolfishly, but the other silenced him with a gesture.

'Only thing,' Chaney said softly, 'he's mine. He killed my old man, I've been training to kill him for seven years, so when he goes down it will be with my bullets in his guts. Savvy?'

They didn't. But they soon did. For both Bo Gaunt and Slinger Dunne had taken remarkably little time to absorb the reality that Chaney Stallard was something very different from themselves, despite their common stock-in-trade. The man radiated danger, exuded a murderous self-assurance – and was plainly not someone a man wanted to wrangle with or disagree with unless there was no option.

The two traded glances. At last Dunne shrugged and spread his hands. He was willing. Bo Gaunt momentarily considered the pleasure of putting six slugs into a man who had chased him halfway across the West, then leaned back in his chair and said, 'I don't give a plug damn who puts him in the ground, so long as I get to dance on his son-of-a-bitch grave!'

Chaney's head bobbed. He had what he wanted. He lighted up and began to speak.

The sheriff swung his swivel-chair around and stared through the bars of the office window at the street.

Main Street, Chad City, still looked the same, he realized.

So, why was he surprised?

It was a rhetorical question, for he knew the answer only too well. It was because a rare period of quiet had prevailed over several days now in the wake of the most recent chapter of bloodshed and drama. He realized he should feel grateful about that, but he didn't. Yet how could any honest lawman sit here and see a man like Jack Stallard strolling along the plankwalk in conversation with a settler from Indian Flats and not feel reassured?

'Too much paper work and not enough pat rolling,' he self-diagnosed. He clamped on his hat and walked out into the sunlight just as Stallard parted from the creeker and came towards him across the street.

The two men greeted one another warmly. The sheriff was a conscientious peace officer with a heart, even if a little unreliable whenever serious trouble erupted. By contrast, the gunfighter was stern and remote by nature yet had proved to be a rock when any ill wind might blow.

They strolled leisurely along Main with the sheriff nodding to this one and that while Stallard stared directly ahead.

The gunfighter was not being aloof; he was simply taking in all he saw and heard while reaching towards a decision.

This was evolving into a period of relative peace, he told himself. Shouldn't he take advantage of that? Move on out and attempt to pick up the stone-cold trail of Bo Gaunt?

Then he realized he'd asked that question of himself both yesterday and the day before that. This meant he was shilly-shallying about going, and that simply was not his style.

He was considering that puzzle when the lawman halted and fingered back his hat.

'I visited with Potter last evening, Mr Stallard. Thought you should know.'

'And?'

'I got the impression he's toned down the past week. You think that could be so?'

'Maybe.'

Stallard was not being deliberately terse. He was only half-listening, his thoughts being focused exclusively on himself at that moment. He knew he felt restless, uncertain and, well, just a tad strange – which was no way for any gunfighter-manhunter to operate.

'You're thinking of going, aren't you?'

He turned sharply. 'Says who?'

'Says my instinct. Well, before you make a decision, I want you to know I'd rather you stayed on, if just for a week or two to see if this period of calm is permanent or not.'

'Want my opinion?'

'Of course.'

'I doubt it is permanent.'

The lawman looked glum. 'What makes you say that?'

Stallard tapped his forehead. 'My experience with sons of bitches, that's what. Potter is successful, clever, has powerful friends and he goes to church Sundays. But underneath he's still a dog. Anyone who would hire a killer like Bloodworth, or order an attack on harmless settlers, is capable of anything. So, just in case I mightn't be here some time, Sheriff, watch Groff Potter.'

With that he was gone, long-striding across the main stem. He was not being unsociable; he'd just sighted a pretty woman entering Miss Jilly's Dresses.

155

Emma acted pleased to see him when he entered the shop, but was restrained, even so. He soon realized why as he watched her attempting to beat down the price on a set of ten knickers, small size, and the same number of poke-bonnets.

'Let me guess,' he said. 'These going to Indian Flats?'

She nodded, but was setting the items back on the show tray when he produced his billfold.

Some twenty minutes later the west side of town sighted Emma Green and the big gun-fighter wheel from the Gimcrack Livery in a rented buckboard, Miss Emma smiling and holding her bonnet on while Mr Stallard, stern looking as usual, plied the reins.

He only appeared to be stern. He'd not realized it was such a fine clear day before, and he was surprised to discover just how good it all felt – the rhythm of the horse, the high sky and fluffy clouds skimming the hill country to the south, the way she smiled when he glanced her way.

OK. Maybe he was smiling because he'd insisted on paying for her purchases, adding a few of his own besides. But he believed she appeared a different girl from the serious one he'd met at the milliner's, was vain enough to hope his company might be responsible for that change.

He silenced the nagging voice that whispered: ladies and gunfighters, Stallard? Who are you trying to fool?

OK. So, if he was fooling himself, it would only be for an hour or two, with no harm done. That silenced the nagging voice and they continued on to the bridge over the creek, then swung down the flats and the timber skeletons of the homes and outbuildings the homesteaders were working on.

Amongst those who paused to greet them was Dad Halliday, who had apparently given himself the post of building overseer. The grandfather appeared to be recovering from the little girl's death the night of the attack, but everywhere he went he toted that outsized Big Fifty rifle, as though to warn everyone the Flats would not be taken unawares a second time.

For his part, Stallard was content to stroll around behind an energetic Emma as she visited the women and children in their lean-tos and tents, and for some two hours the gunfighter was more relaxed than he could ever recall being, certainly not since he'd tucked a wanted poster on one Bo Gaunt and followed a trail south-west.

But that dodger was still in his pocket, and that backshooting killer was down south ... somewhere...

They were quiet on the drive home in the twilight, but it was silence with depth to it. She sat closer on the high seat than she had done on the drive out, and he sensed he might have put an arm around her shoulders without offending.

But he didn't. They were heading into the outskirts of town now and yard by yard, reality was returning.

She fixed coffee for them both at the office. They sat in silence for a time. Then she said, 'You are still intending to move on, aren't you?'

He admitted this was so. This was not some sort of game. He only had to look into her eyes and feel the tightness in his chest to know that.

She did not attempt to get him to change his mind, and he sensed strongly that he would have liked it had she done so. She moved on from that awkward moment to bring him abreast of the local gossip and her plans for the future for Indian Flats. And for a time Jack Stallard willingly allowed himself go along with the fantasy of what it must be like to be just a regular man – hard-working, settled, no taste for drama or danger. Married and settled, no doubt? No doubt.

He then realized she was rising to leave. 'Another?' he heard himself say.

Her smile was warm but maybe a little weary. 'You don't need caffeine to keep you on the go, Jack Stallard. You need to be going right now, I can see it in your eyes. I'm sorry, I think I was hoping...'

He never did find out what it was she might be hoping. She was gone in a moment. He stood outside on the walk, watching her figure recede, and knew a moment of true pain.

But it didn't last long, and shortly he was striding along the plankwalk with all his old energy and vigour again. For a moment back there he'd felt some loco impulse to seize her by the hands and say some crazy thing that he would only have had to take back later.

By the time he'd reached the corner he knew he would quit Chad City within the next forty-eight hours. He told himself he could already feel the thrill of the hunt and hear the familiar sounds of the wide open spaces.

But he also knew what a lie sounded like when he heard one.

CHAPTER 10

ALWAYS THE GUNS

Like an old lion confined to its cage, Groff Potter sulked and growled and rejected all company, whether it be friendly, hostile or somewhere in that grey area in between.

It wasn't easy to give in to self-pity and bitter anger in the lush comfort of that huge house on the southern slope of the ranch's Mesquite Hill, just above the eastern fringe of Chad City.

Locals often pointed out the Slash K headquarters with pride to visitors, and with good reason. There was nothing to match it in the county and it seemed to impart a sense of permanence and pride to the entire town, even to those who hated their most powerful cattleman and citizen like a rat hates red pepper.

The mansion had always been his comfort and reassurance, but not tonight. Slumped in a deep leather chair with glass in hand and a bottle within reach, the big man was deliberately coming up with one negative after another tonight.

There seemed to be no shortage of them, and he could list and consider several of the weightier irritants without half trying. But right up near the top of his list, as it mostly was these days, was the homesteader threat. Just a week earlier he'd appeared to be getting on top of those johnny-come-lately claim-jumping nobodies who'd been making his life a misery. He'd had some judges supporting him, a number of influential town identities, even some of Chad City's poor, who seemed to fear that more poor coming in would only make their lives harder.

He'd also boasted a strong workforce and a gang of almost-legal enforcers on his payroll. He had fully expected that by now the invaders would have been run off Indian Flats, with the law ensuring that they stayed away, leaving clear sailing ahead for the Potter Stock And Beef Company.

Seemed like a dream now – or a nightmare.

The raid on the Flats and the reaction to it had hit back hard and was still hurting like hell. The town council had reacted badly, the homesteaders, though wounded, had stood their ground and fought back, and even that lousy rag they called a newspaper was attacking both Potter and his raid in its columns.

Then he'd lost his temper and kicked Slinger Dunne off the place and nobody seemed capable of keeping either his security force or his ranch hands properly in check since.

What a crock!

Heavy oaken doors creaked open and a head peered round the edge. 'You got visitors, Mr Potter sir.'

'Tell them to die!'

'Er ... not just regular visitors, sir. Mr Dunne is one, you see.'

'That flash bastard!' he snarled, yet found himself sitting more upright as he frowned hard and ran a hand over his big-nosed face. 'I told him to get the hell and I meant–'

'He ain't alone, boss. You might be cheered some to see who he's got with him.'

'All right, all right, show them all in. All the more for me to boot out on their lousy fat–'

He broke off abruptly as Slinger Dunne entered the room like he owned it. The cattleman was about to welcome him with a curse when two total strangers followed, showing no greater fear or respect than the gunslinger had done.

Potter stared.

One man was a formidable six-footer with square shoulders and a mighty hard eye. But the third man looked like a bum in trail-stained denim, his features gnarled and vicious in the lantern-glow. This one sported two sixguns strapped around narrow hips and seemed to exude an odd kind of natural authority even as he moved past the first two to halt squarely before Potter's big chair.

'What the Sam Hill?' Potter rumbled, heaving his long lean body erect. 'And just who and what in hell might you be, sir?'

'The name is Stallard. That's the who. The what is, I'm the man who can solve your biggest problem the only way anyone can.' The man's shoulder dipped and a sixgun filled his hand so fast it caused Potter to reel back against his chair in shock. 'With this!' He pulled trigger and the hammer fell upon an empty chamber, causing the rancher's heart to leap in his chest. 'Well, grandad, ain't you going to say something?'

Potter would have plenty to say – when he caught his breath. And when at last this evil old man smiled, it was a frightening thing to see.

There had been no warning – not to Jack

Stallard nor anybody else.

It had been a quiet morning on Main Street, with folks going about their everyday chores and nothing unusual or special about the Glory Road saloon for that matter: a few porch loafers, the mailman pausing at one end to check out his letters, a creaking wagon rolling by and raising dust as Stallard came out of Walker Street and swung right.

The first thing he grew aware of was the sudden hush that seemed to fall clear across the street. Then he heard a shocked voice gasp, 'My God – my God ... no!' and that brought him wheeling about sharply to look towards the saloon.

And there they were.

Slinger Dunne and Bo Gaunt were positioned wide of the swinging doors, facing him, and standing on the very front edge of the thirty-foot front gallery, was the deadly figure of his brother!

His hand slapped gun handle but he did not draw. Not yet. He was certain what this had to be, yet he must be sure.

'You!' he heard himself gasp. 'What–'

'No jawbone, brother.' Chaney's voice was even deeper and more harsh, if that were possible. He seemed to radiate a superhuman assurance, standing there with hands fanned

164

over gun handles, a demonic intensity. 'Since the day you murdered my old man, you've known this day would come … and it is here. So draw and die, you piece of dirt!'

And four sets of hands clawed for their guns.

In a lifetime with the guns Jack Stallard was never faster. He knew it as he went into his draw, was totally certain of it as his palms slapped gun handles and his Peacemakers leapt from the leather in one blurred split second of perfect co-ordination of mind, muscle and eye.

Yet his brother beat him to it.

The stunning realization came with a great billow of gunsmoke obscuring Chaney's upper body followed instantly by the thundering racket of the shot and the venomous airwhip of the bullet going past his cheekbone.

Chaney had beaten him to it – and missed!

Instantly Jack's heavy Colt spewed fire and smoke and his brother was driven backwards to crash into the wall of the saloon and go down.

Lunging violently to one side, Jack went low and fast and fanned his gun hammer to loose a thundering fusillade at the tall form of Bo Gaunt who took the murderous volley squarely in the chest before he could even squeeze trigger, slamming him to the plankboards with such force that the body rolled three times before it came to rest.

Nobody spared the dead man a glance. Every eye was on the men still on their feet and in the shaved tip of a second, Jack Stallard was struck.

The bullet from Slinger Dunne's .44-.40 ripped his shoulder and sent him spinning and dropping a Colt. A woman screamed but nobody heard. Gun thunder ruled the towering moment, and hunting lead stitched a lethal pattern of pursuit in the deep dust of the street as Jack spun violently left, then right.

Dunne's hammer clicked on an empty chamber with a slight sound that was scarcely noticed by anybody except a bloodied but iron-jawed Jack Stallard.

Who was up on one knee and shooting back.

Dunne had his second .45 sweeping to cover him when the first bullet struck. Handsome Slinger lost every last vestige of colour in the space of one heartbeat. He had his gun level and aimed but did not shoot. He stared at the fast-rising Stallard, his broad brow furrowed in confusion, as though he could not understand the roar of the crowd, the light rushing out of the sky – none of it.

He whirled in a slow pirouette and plunged off the porchboards face downwards in the dust.

Jack didn't spare him a glance. There was no time. He flicked one glance at Bo Gaunt who appeared to be slumped against a bloodstained wall. Instantly he swung his head to peer through the gunsmoke clouding the saloon gallery. There was movement along the gallery; he heard himself groan aloud when he sighted through the dust and roiling gunsmoke the figure of his brother out on the street, fifty yards distant, upright and gun in hand, face fearsome in its total hatred.

Chaney triggered and missed – for the second time. Nobody realized the killer had lead in him someplace. Someone cheered and another voice from the ranks of the homesteaders screamed, 'Finish him off, Mister Jack! He's sick as a dog!'

Standing weaving with boots wide-planted, Jack barely heard. He could barely hear at all, while the saloon rippled in his vision as though it was under water. His gun was held at shooting level, had been for several seconds, of which each moment seemed minutes long in this unbearable tension. He attempted to jerk trigger but his gun remained silent. For now the figure leaning towards him with his pistol at firing-level was not his brother but his father ... and he was fifteen years of age on the worst day of his life ... and his father was falling before his gun with eyes already locked in death.

'Shoot! Shoot! Shoot!'

It was a desperate chant rising from a score of throats – suddenly a hundred. Yet Jack Stallard continued to stand there shrouded by smoke and dust, staring upwards across at his brother and watching the finger whitening on the trigger, the wolf-grin of total, savagery and triumph.

'Pure yellow underneath and I always knew it – *brother!*' Chaney screamed, trembling with hate and pain, but triumphant. 'So go straight to hell–'

His words were swallowed by a sound. It was a towering thunderclap of a sound that erupted from of the homesteader ranks and came blasting out of the gun muzzle of a Big Fifty rifle clutched in the gnarled hands of Homer Strong – those sure and vengeful hands of one old man who still had courage, who still could fight.

Jack Stallard slowly lowered his revolver

and watched his brother's death dive into the deep dust of the street.

Instantly the street was hushed, with every eye upon the old nester as he came forward toting the still smoking rifle to stand by Stallard, whose face was grey. While up on the gallery, men had hold of flashy Bo Gaunt whose nerve had failed him just when it mattered most.

'This man!' Homer Strong announced in a booming voice that carried, 'went through the hell of killing his father to stop him killing him and his mother, whom he loved.' He paused to boost his rifle above his head. 'Killing somebody of your own blood is something no man, neither good nor bad, should ever have to go through in this life. But to be called on to do it again? I couldn't see that happen to nobody, and I just made certain sure I didn't!'

It seemed a long, taut time before the sheriff emerged from the silent crowd and walked across to inspect the dead.

The day the trials finally wound up coincided with the first real blast of winter. Overnight the valley felt the first of the biting winds that came down from the Hard Luck Hills, and the women spilling from the rickety old court house-cum-dance-hall on the main street south were decked out in bright woollen weather coats and gaudy hatwear, their menfolk more serious and sober in leather, denim and big Western hats.

It was all vivid and sharp to the eye of Jack Stallard, standing rolling a cigarette with his back turned against the wind in the centre of a group of well-wishers, which included a number of ragged settlers from Indian Flats.

It had taken time to recover from the murderous business of that day a month ago now. The dust had settled, and though there was still pain, he knew it would pass.

The judge's final findings were largely responsible for the prevailing good mood evident on all sides right now, while the ten-year stretch in the county jail for Groff Potter had been greeted with cheers inside.

Of course, when something as violent as the events that had marked the valley's last days of summer and fall erupted any place, there was always a great amount of recovery, bridge-building and goodwill required to ensure that any region might go forward and not regress.

Much was already clearer than it had been, but there was plainly a great deal yet to be done. Dragging deeply on his roll-your-own and listening to Emma and her cousins discussing events, he was too preoccupied with the here and now to be overly concerned about the future of the town, or himself for that matter. As a consequence he wasn't aware of the approach of the sheriff and judge until they were standing before him.

'Old Fifty-Five' was holding forth, but fell silent when he realized they were in exalted company. The circuit judge was a fierce old justice, yet at the moment was wearing an almost benign expression – for some reason or other.

That reason became clear when the sheriff began to talk. He and the judge had been holding regular discussions over the past several evenings, he explained, and the upshot of these dialogues had been an agreement that, despite the break-up of Slash K and an atmosphere of relative peace, Chad City very plainly required an upgrade where law enforcement was concerned.

Jack was nodding in silent agreement when the bombshell dropped.

'We'd like you to take on the job of special deputy, Jack,' said the sheriff. The man waited until the shock began to recede from Stallard's face, then added the kicker. 'The judge is prepared to authorize it, I'd welcome it one hundred per cent...' Here he paused to smile fatuously. 'And Miss Green approves. Ain't that right, Miss Green?'

'Quite right,' Emma agreed brightly, giving Stallard's arm a squeeze. Then, searching the gunfighter's face, she added hastily, 'But I do think Jack would appreciate a little time to think it over, wouldn't you, Jack?'

It took him a fortnight, the first ten days of which were spent largely locked in disagreeing with Emma, old Homer, the sheriff and many of the towners regarding the loco proposal he'd been given. Yet that last few days brought a change that came about when the law office in Parlo mailed him an assignment to drop whatever he was doing and go after the Dalton Gang.

He would still like to see the Daltons finished, yet the moment he began considering the proposal, he envisioned what it must entail. A long hunt, danger every mile, and if it proved successful – surely blood and guns at the end of it.

And that was the notion and the image that did it for Jack Stallard, ex-bounty hunter. For it was not until that moment that he realized fully just what effect that murderous gun battle had had. Three men dead, one a brother. That surely was not simply enough, it went far beyond that. All the way in fact to Jack Stallard, former gunfighter, enquiring of judge and sheriff whether it would be feasible and possible to become the kind of peace officer you saw more and more back in the East these days; the ones equipped with a baton, not guns.

He left the two men debating his proposal soberly, and took Emma by the arm to make his first ever totally relaxed way along Main Street, Chad City. In the blustery wind and the beginning of a thin cold rain, he knew he would take their job if they made the concession, but also knew he would not really care if they did not. For the only change that really signified was, not how he might make his living now he'd hung up the guns, but how quickly and smoothly he might now get to erase the old and embrace the new.

Emma looked up at him as they passed Smiggert's Corner, and he sensed he might be almost there already.

The publishers hope that this book has given you enjoyable reading. Large Print Books are especially designed to be as easy to see and hold as possible. If you wish a complete list of our books please ask at your local library or write directly to:

Dales Large Print Books
Magna House, Long Preston,
Skipton, North Yorkshire.
BD23 4ND

This Large Print Book, for people
who cannot read normal print,
is published under the auspices of

THE ULVERSCROFT FOUNDATION

... we hope you have enjoyed this book.
Please think for a moment about those
who have worse eyesight than you ...
and are unable to even read or enjoy
Large Print without great difficulty.

You can help them by sending a
donation, large or small, to:

**The Ulverscroft Foundation,
1, The Green, Bradgate Road,
Anstey, Leicestershire, LE7 7FU,
England.**
or request a copy of our brochure for
more details.

The Foundation will use all donations
to assist those people who are visually
impaired and need special attention
with medical research, diagnosis
and treatment.

Thank you very much for your help.